I0822400

#MANLOVE

CAMBRIA ***HEBERT***

Published by Cambria Hebert
http://www.cambriahebert.com

Cover design by Cover Me Darling
Cover Art by David DaSilva
Edited by Cassie McCown
Interior formatting by: Classic Interior Design

To all those who said that if I wrote a MM novel, it would ruin my career.

You were wrong.

And to all those who proved it by making Trent & Drew one of my most-loved couples... and for keeping their love alive for the last decade.

You are iconic.

#trewlove forever

#MANLOVE

Racing's most talked-about couple is back!

Not that they ever really left.

Drew Mask has achieved legendary status since New Revolution Racing was founded—a division he helped pioneer.

A division filled with underdogs that many said would crash and burn before it even got started.

Well, it's been over a decade since no-rules racing debuted, and it's hotter than ever with no plan to hit the brakes anytime soon.

But what about Mask? Since hurtling into the spotlight, this most-loved professional street racer has won a mind-boggling number of championships, amassed an astonishing list of division records, and become the most decorated and accomplished driver in the NRR.

Incredible feats, most of which he accomplished after a near-fatal crash.

Perhaps, though, what makes Drew Mask truly a legend is that his influence extends beyond his driving career. He and his hottie of a husband, Trent, have been an iconic force in normalizing same-sex relationships in professional sports.

So when whispers of retirement made it to our ears here at GearShark, we decided it was time to catch up with our favorite couple to see how they've managed to balance it all while keeping their #manlove alive and, of course, if those rumors of retirement are fake news or verified.

Full article inside...

#MANLOVE

A GEAR*SHARK* SERIES NOVELLA

CAMBRIA *HEBERT*

1

Drew

A cloud of dust hung in our wake and small rocks dinged the undercarriage as the Fastback went from zero to sixty in impressively quick time. The back end fishtailed a bit, and the knuckles of the hands wrapped around the steering wheel turned white, ready to strong-arm her back in line.

From the driver's seat, Trav darted a glance in my direction, and I grinned. "Faster!"

With a *whoop,* he dropped a hand onto the gearshift and punched it forward, the rumble of the engine deepening in response. We flew over the dirt road, wind whipping through the open windows tugging at our hair and clothes as the scent of dirt and gasoline filled the air.

God, I love this.

And even though we were flying down the road, going definitely faster than I should allow, time seemed to slow. As everything around us blurred out of focus, I lived in a moment of perfect clarity. And in the center was my son. Jaw set in determination, ring-covered fingers gripping the wheel as black strands of hair blew everywhere. Even with black aviators shading his eyes, I knew without a doubt those onyx orbs were narrowed as he scrutinized the road ahead.

I was no longer the only adrenaline junkie in this family. It was a title I now shared with my son.

God, I love this kid.

Feeling my attention, he turned his face, and our eyes connected. The corner of his mouth tilted up before he turned back to refocus.

Up ahead, the road curved, and I patted on the dashboard, pointing. "Remember what I told you," I yelled over the engine and blowing wind.

He nodded once.

My pulse hammered with anticipation as I grabbed the door handle to hang on. Travis downshifted, and even though the Mustang slowed, my heart rate didn't. Just when I thought he overshot, Travis flicked the wheel, pulled the e-brake, and then pumped the clutch to destabilize the back wheels. The car started to slide.

"Increase the throttle," I hollered. Then, "Back off just a little."

The car drifted around the turn, arching almost perfectly. I felt Trav lighten up on the gas pedal—a natural instinct but not the right move.

"Keep that foot down." I reminded him, and he pushed down, the car finishing out the drift perfectly.

Pride filled my chest when he flicked the wheel in the opposite direction, let off the gas at the exact right moment, and shot forward.

Hollering, I dropped my arm out of the window to slap on the door. "Fucking right!" I roared.

Trav's face transformed into a wide grin, and I knew

another slowed-down moment of clarity. The joy on his face and sense of accomplishment filling the cab were something I wanted to remember forever.

I grabbed my phone and snapped a pic for Trent, wanting to share it with him.

In true dramatic fashion, Trav hit the brakes and spun in a three-sixty before coming to a complete stop in the center of a dust cloud. I coughed and waved away some of the polluted air, pushing my hair off my forehead.

"Well?" Trav asked, looking at me for approval.

"You sure like waiting to the very last second," I joked.

He smirked as though he did it on purpose, which he probably did.

Laughing under my breath, I palmed his shoulder. "That was your best drift yet," I said. "You're a damn good driver, son."

"Good enough for my own car?"

I groaned. This kid had been working on Trent and me for his own car since he was fourteen.

Did you hear me say *fourteen?*

Probably why I was starting to see some silver in my scruff. Wasn't at all because I was now in my forties. It was these kids for sure.

Obviously, we told him no.

So he took one of the four-wheelers out one day when we weren't looking and crashed it into a tree about a mile from the house.

It didn't matter that he jumped off before the crash. Or that his injuries were minor. When he limped into the house, bloodied and bruised, I nearly lost my shit.

Thank God Trent was there. The man had a backbone made of steel. Even though I saw the ghosts from my accident nearly twelve years before haunting his eyes, he acted like they weren't there as he took control of the situation and protected me from the PTSD threatening to take over.

Actually, pretty sure he sucked it right out of me with a mind-numbing blow job.

Yep, I still loved a good blow job.

Trav got grounded. He also had to pay for all the parts to fix the quad, which he earned by doing chores for his aunts. Once he made enough for the new parts, he had to help fix it. Though, it didn't deter him from wanting to drive. If anything, it made him more eager. He liked being under the hood with an engine just as much as he liked being behind the wheel.

We decided it was best for me to teach him how to handle a car because at least then he'd have skills to protect himself and wouldn't be out trying to teach himself and crashing into shit.

Now here we were, a week shy of his seventeenth birthday. Well, maybe lessons on drifting weren't necessary, but it sure as hell was fun.

Travis was a natural driver, better than I was at that age.

'Course, maybe if my dad had taken an interest in my love for driving back then, I would have been. But we don't need to talk about that.

"I did see an ad for a nice four-cylinder Honda the other day," I mused.

Travis gave me a *cut the shit* look—did I mention teenagers have attitude for daysss?—and curled his lip. "I could run faster than a four-cylinder."

"Maybe you should quit football and join the track team," I cracked.

He didn't think it was funny. "*Dad.*"

I laughed at his insufferable tone.

"It was brand new." I defended the Honda.

"Even worse," he spat. "It probably has all that driving assist shit."

"Watch your mouth," I warned.

Look, just because I dropped an F-bomb back there in the heat of the moment doesn't mean we let our kids cuss.

He rolled his eyes.

I had to resist rolling mine back.

"I don't want a car that drives me. I want to be the one in control."

I respected it. I even thought it was smart. In my humble opinion, modern cars didn't require as much skill because they had lane assist, parking assist, hands-free driving, etc. And yeah, the safety features were great, and it was good for kids new to driving. Hell, really anyone who couldn't drive for shit, which was eighty percent of the people on the road.

But.

If we let cars do everything, then how were they supposed to learn? Hell, they don't even teach cursive in schools these days. Kids see cursive now and act like it's a foreign language. I had to teach my son how to sign his name. And there's this app where you take a photo of your math homework and it does it for you.

What kind of BS is that? I would have loved that shit when I was in high school, but I'm not in high school. I'm a parent. I got to make sure my kid knows how to survive.

I let him use that math app, though. Since when do you need advanced algebra to survive?

Exactly. You don't.

I lifted my eyebrows. "Need I remind you of the quad incident?"

Travis made a rude sound. "That was three years ago."

"Two and a half." I corrected him.

"I'm a way better driver now. I've had my license for over a year."

Some of that was a learner's permit, but I didn't bother pointing it out. To him, it was all the same. Instead, I said, "Having your own car is a lot of responsibility."

"Whatever," he grumbled, reaching for the ignition.

"Hey," I said, leaning over to grasp his arm.

He shook me off.

"Travis," I said in a much firmer tone, my hand going back to his arm.

"What?" he answered, impatient.

"You know what."

He said nothing.

"Son."

He blew out a breath. "Don't drive angry." He repeated what I'd told him many times before. He glanced at me, then away. "It clouds your judgment and makes you do stupid things."

"Just like drinking and driving," I added.

He rolled his eyes. "*I know.*"

I deserved it, but I gotta be his dad, not his friend. Even though I really wanted to be his friend. My son was hella cool.

"We know you want your own car. We just want to make sure you're ready. We want you to be safe."

"I'll be safe, Dad." He met my eyes. "I swear."

A lump formed in my throat. It felt like just yesterday he called me Dad for the first time, and now I was teaching him to drive and trying to hold on to him just a little longer. I was good with speed, but damn, time went by too fast.

"How about you drive us up to the main house?" I said, motioning to the dirt track Trent and I made deep in the property on our family compound. It was originally for the ATVs, but it turned out it was also great for all the up-and-coming teens in this fam learning to drive. "If we're late for pancake Sunday, you won't need a car because your aunts will murder us," I joked.

Trav drove us across the compound until the dirt road met the paved one and the main house came into view. He didn't drive fast or do any stunts, and he used his turn signal every time even though we were the only car out here. I knew he was showing me he was a good driver and capable of being responsible. My head already knew he was ready. My heart, though... In my heart, he was still a little boy running around with my phone, catching Pokémon.

Trent was standing on the wide steps of the front porch when Travis pulled up. My eyes went to him immediately, the tension coiling inside me loosening at just the sight of him.

We'd been together over a decade, but the way he always affected me felt brand new. All those years ago, in the beginning, it was a tight bond of friendship, of being comfortable with someone and knowing he had my back. Then our bond deepened into something more possessive, something intense I didn't want to share. Suddenly, his presence gave me butterflies and a hum of anticipation beneath my skin. I still think about that first kiss and the way he slid his hand down my arm, acknowledging the way I trembled as he laced our fingers. That kiss changed my entire life, turning our friendship into something stronger, something I knew I would never live without.

And then came death.

I learned I wouldn't die without him either.

We became fate. Inevitable in every way, in every scenario. There will never be a tomorrow when we aren't together because that day could never exist.

Cheesy as fuck, I know. But not even I could deny it when I saw him standing there waiting.

Travis parked the Fastback a few feet from the steps, cut

the engine, and tugged the keys from the ignition. Forcing my eyes from my husband, I turned toward our son.

"You did good today."

"How good?" he needled, handing me the keys.

I shook my head, amused. "I'll talk to your dad, okay?"

His onyx eyes sparked with hope. "Really?"

"Have I ever lied to you?"

"Whoop!" he hollered, bounding out of the driver's seat, slamming the heavy door. He jogged up the stairs two at a time and then stopped in front of his dad. He was a pretty tall kid, but Trent was bigger, and it did something to my heart to see Trav tip his head back and smile up at him.

Trent's mouth moved, and then Travis nodded. They pounded it out, and Trav went inside, leaving the front door wide open.

Clearly, he didn't pay the electric bill.

The second he disappeared, Trent rotated, our eyes met, and my stomach dipped.

We stayed like that for long moments, him at the top of the stairs and me leaning against the car while early autumn air mixed with the end of summer sun, creating a seasonal tug of war between us.

The invisible tether connecting us pulled eagerly, but I stayed rooted in place, wanting to anticipate him just a moment longer.

God, I love him. He was practically my definition of love.

His head tilted just a little, and I pushed off the car and strode forward, breaking into a jog and bounding up the stairs. He opened his arms, and I leaped into them, wrapping my legs around his narrow waist and my arms around his neck.

This is exactly where I belong.

A deliciously deep growl vibrated his throat, and he

turned, pinning me against the side of the house. "*Baby*," he rumbled before capturing my mouth in a possessive kiss.

I gripped his wide shoulders. The warmth of his bare skin seeped into my palms, raring to life the infinite hunger I had for him. Gliding down, I delved beneath the edges of his damp tank, fingertips slipping across sweat-slicked skin. I swear this man only got sexier with age. Beneath the tank, I palmed his defined pecks, groping every inch and smearing the sweat gathered between them. His body shifted, hand coming up to collar the back of my neck and squeeze. The ownership in that action drew a needy sound right out of me.

He smirked, the arrogant bastard, but I didn't call him on it because he gave me no time. The smirk slipped away the second his mouth claimed mine. The kiss was deep but slow and deliberate, making my thoughts go fuzzy and heat pulse through my veins. My fingers sank into his rippling back muscles, and I arched closer, his hand moving to cradle the back of my head while he bulldozed what was left of my thoughts with his skilled tongue.

Growling, Trent ripped his mouth free to kiss across my stubbled jaw, making low noises of appreciation and latching on to my neck. I hissed at the pleasure-pain combo when he sucked deep, rocking my hips into his midsection for some friction on my rigid dick.

He released my neck and lifted his head, and I fell onto him, feral, with a growl of my own, pushing my face into his neck to breathe deep the musky scent of sweat. When that wasn't enough, I dragged my tongue over his salty and sticky skin, humming with satisfaction.

Grunting, Trent yanked my hair, forcing my head up so he could kiss me again, this time more urgently than the last.

"It's a good thing we don't have neighbors because they'd

have called the cops by now." Braeden's voice cut into the desire binding us.

Trent's lips gentled, and I made a disgruntled, almost desperate sound because I wasn't ready to let him go. His smile was wolfish when he came back, our lips meeting again. I pushed closer, forgetting all about Braeden.

"You ever thought about doing OnlyFans?"

He was like a gnat, always hovering. Annoying everyone.

Trent laughed, the movement breaking the kiss. Breathless, I glared over his shoulder at my dear brother standing in the open doorway.

He held up his hands defensively. "Just saying, you two love PDA. Might as well make some cash off it."

"As if Drew would ever let anyone stare at Trent," Romeo quipped, appearing from inside the house.

Oh, look, an infestation of gnats.

"If the price was right..." B said, letting his words trail away.

I gave them both the finger. "Fuck off."

Ever since I nearly died all those years ago, we stopped giving a damn about PDA and worrying what people might think about our affection, but Braeden had to be putting whisky in his coffee if he thought I'd ever share Trent.

Mmm, coffee.

"Breakfast is in ten. Better go shower off," Romeo said. "The girls will complain if you come to the table fresh from a workout."

That explained Trent's deliciously sweaty attire.

"And with a raging boner," Braeden muttered.

I stiffened and looked down. I was still in Trent's arms, legs around his waist. His body was definitely blocking my *raging boner.* There was no way anyone could see.

Braeden made a rude sound. "Don't bother denying it.

You've been humping him like a dog in heat since I came out here."

Shocked, my eyes flew to Trent whose shoulders began vibrating with contained laughter. His glittering hazel eyes were oh so smug. Cheeks hot, I buried my face in the side of his neck with a groan.

"Don't be embarrassed. We're all dudes here." Braeden just kept talking. "We'll cover with the girls. And keep the kids occupied. Go get some of that man love."

Braeden's and Romeo's laughter faded as they went back into the house, but I kept my face pressed into T. He must have been releasing some extra pheromones or something from that workout because he smelled hella good.

Chuckling, he stepped back, and I tightened my arms around him, making a sound of denial.

"I got you, Mask." His voice was deep, low, and right beside my ear. Tingles fired across my scalp and pebbled the skin on my arms.

The front door slammed when he kicked it shut behind us, and instead of heading toward the dining room, he carried me up the stairs. His body shifted with every step, and his midsection rubbed teasingly against my still-hard cock.

I nibbled on his neck, practically vibrating with how bad I wanted him.

Another door closed, followed immediately by the sound of a lock.

Oh, fuck yes.

Moments later, I was being pulled away from his chest, my back meeting something solid. Startled, I glanced around, then back to T, surprised.

"Stand on the bar, baby."

I didn't know what it was about that word, but it hit

different when he called me that. It turned me into some sort of simp.

So much so that I didn't even question why he wanted me to step onto the inversion table, which was standing straight up. I stepped onto the small foot bar and leaned against the padded table. Trent bent immediately to engage the locks, closing the padded clamps around my ankles. Once those were secure, he stepped close, slipping his fingertips beneath the hem of my shirt.

"Lift."

My arms rose on command, and he stripped off my shirt, throwing it over his shoulder. My tongue darted out, wetting my lips, when he reached for the button on my jeans, flicking it open in a second flat and then slowly dragging the zipper down.

He leaned in, lips hovering over mine, and my breath hitched. I swayed forward, but then he was gone, yanking both the jeans and boxers down to just below my knees.

I jolted in surprise, hands wrapping around the handles of the table as cool air brushed over my heated skin, cock jerking in response.

"Look at you," Trent murmured, dragging his fingers from my knees all the way to the top of my thighs. "Why so needy, baby?"

My eyes swept over him. The maroon tank exposed his massive shoulders and the sides of his torso. The black shorts he wore molded to his thick thighs, not loose enough to hide the bulge he was rocking.

His skin was dewy with sweat, and I knew his hands would be calloused from lifting weights.

"Touch me already," I spat.

Chuckling, he stepped forward.

"Lose the shirt," I demanded, already breathless.

He tore it over his head, abs rippling with the movement.

He had a good pump going on since he'd just been lifting, and the veins running down his arms had my teeth sinking into my lip.

The world tilted, feet coming out from under me, making all the air in my lungs whoosh out. Gripping the handles, I glanced down, seeing that Trent had tilted the table so I was lying flat on my back.

"What are you doing, frat boy?" I asked, looking up his bare upper body as he towered over me.

"Strapping you down so I can have my way with you," he replied, reaching down to wrap his hand around my shaft. "You got a problem with that?"

I shook my head profusely.

Laughing under his breath, he stroked me, his firm and confident hand making my eyes roll back in my head.

The world tilted again, and my eyes reopened, finding the world upside down. I wasn't completely upside down, but my feet and legs were higher than my head, leaving me completely vulnerable and exposed.

Before I could think too much about it, T leaned in and swallowed me down. I groaned lewdly, remembering partway through that we were at the main house, in the family gym. I used my hand to muffle the sounds escaping my mouth as he took me into his throat.

The man was a master at a BJ, his powers of deepthroating something I literally dreamed about. He dragged his lips back and swirled around my tip, flirting with my glans before locking his lips around the swollen tip to suck.

My shoulders came off the table, and I gripped the handlebars until my finger joints ached. Trent pulled back and sucked me down again, grabbing the table and pushing so my dick was forced the deepest it had ever been in his throat.

I cursed. The feel of his tight throat spasming around me almost had me shooting off just then. I swear I saw stars, and when he rocked the table ever so slightly, tears sprang to my eyes.

"*Trent*." His name was a guttural, broken sound, and my dick was so far down his throat he couldn't reply. I wanted to tell him not to hurt himself, but damn, I was too far gone.

The tight fit, the slight thrusting motion, and the way he instinctively tried to swallow around me were more than I could take.

Forgetting the handlebars, I wrapped my arm around his leg, hugging tight.

He pulled back a little, gasping for breath, and then dove back on, settling into a rhythm that was nothing but sweet torture. My fingernails pricked the skin on his legs. I strained against the ankle cuffs, and he wrapped those big, calloused hands around the backs of my thighs and squeezed.

I erupted with a shout, my entire body locking up as waves of unparalleled pleasure crashed over me again and again. I moaned, thighs trembling as he worked me through the orgasm, milking me for every last drop. And when I collapsed back against the table, my arms falling slack against my sides, he closed his fist around my shaft and licked the head like an ice cream cone.

Spots swam before my vision, and my breathing was uneven. Now that my dick was spent, all the blood pooled in my head, leaving me dizzy and warm. I blinked at the sound of rustling clothing and watched T push his shorts down to just below his ass.

I reached forward, my arm weak and trembling. He laughed under his breath and pushed my arm back, tipping the table so I was more upright and even with his angry, red cock.

"Stick out your tongue, baby."

I turned my cheek and did as he asked, opening wide and offering my tongue.

The muscle in his forearm bulged, the vein in his bicep popping as he worked his dick right next to my waiting tongue. The sound of his labored breathing filled the space above my head.

His hips jerked, movements stalling, and I leaned over to swipe over his tip.

With a throaty groan, Trent unleashed. Ropes of white cum shot out, splattering my tongue and lips. I lapped at it as he gave himself a final pump, the last of his release shooting across my cheek.

Quiet blanketed the room as our uneven breathing calmed and the hunger we knew for each other was temporarily sated.

Palming the side of the table, Trent adjusted it so I was upright and unlatched the restraints at my ankles. My entire body still felt like Jell-O and I didn't trust my legs, so I remained where I was until he reached for me.

I moved into his arms, letting him lift me down and into a hug. His breath ruffled the hair on the side of my head, and the skin on his shoulder was warm beneath my cheek.

"I love you." His voice was raspy from how far he'd had my dick down his throat.

I kissed his shoulder and tightened my arms. "We should take that table home."

He let out an amused grunt. "Braeden would never let us live it down."

I snuggled closer. "Worth it."

His silent laughter vibrated through me as his rough palm rubbed up my back and found its way into the uncombed strands of my hair.

"Tell me what happened, baby." His voice was even and patient.

Of course he knew. Trent *always* knew. He possessed some sort of intuition no one else did. A sixth sense when it came to me and our kids.

"You were outside waiting," I said quietly, not bothering to lift my cheek from his shoulder.

"I saw the Fastback coming up the road from the window."

"We should shower," I said. "I can't go downstairs with your jizz in my scruff."

"Are you stalling?" he asked.

Was I? Not really because I knew I'd tell him. I told Trent everything. "No, I'm just not done with you yet."

He swept me off my feet and walked into the adjoining bathroom. "I'll wash your back."

"Is that all?" I complained, looping my arms around his neck. After my accident, T got in the habit of carrying me around and never really stopped. Never thought I'd be the type to like it, but I did. Something about it just made me feel safe.

He laughed. "Now, baby, you know damn well that once I get my hands on you, they'll be everywhere."

2

Trent

The shower was much shorter than I wanted it to be, but with the entire family waiting because of our long-standing pancake Sunday tradition, I couldn't linger—no matter how tempting it was.

'Course, with my husband all needy and naked, I didn't exactly hurry either.

Drew might be all *fries before guys,* but I was more *nudes before foods.*

He was in even less of a hurry than me, still standing there dripping wet with a towel gripped loosely in his fist while I was already dried off with a fresh pair of sweats covering my lower half.

"I haven't had enough coffee yet, frat boy," Drew grumped, water-logged hair dripping into his eyes.

Holding in a laugh, I took the towel and tossed it over his head. "You are such a procrastinator," I mused, gently drying off his overly long strands. Drew was permanently in need of a haircut and shave, and I was permanently turned on by both.

I laughed at the strands sticking up all over the place, the new silver looking near white. Lucky for him, he was blond, so the gray didn't age him, just made him blonder.

Working my way down his body, I dried him thoroughly, going as far as sinking to my knees to get his lower half. He hummed appreciatively, fingers delving into my damp hair, which I'd already combed. Tingles raced across my scalp and down the back of my neck from the touch, and I took a little longer than necessary to dry his calves and feet because the feel of his hands was my addiction.

The second I pulled back, his voice filled the bathroom. "You missed a spot."

Amused, I raised my eyebrows, silently asking where. He pointed to a rogue waterdrop high on his chest, so I used the corner of the towel to mop it up.

He pointed to another on his collarbone.

One on his neck.

Puckered his lips and pointed there too.

My stomach dropped as if I wasn't standing on solid ground because this man—*my husband*—had the innate ability to rock my world with the simplest of gestures.

Playing along, I brushed the soft towel across his lower lip.

His hand flew up, wrapping around my wrist to squeeze. Our eyes met, and the towel fell from my hand as I roped my arm around him and tugged, bringing us chest to chest and mouth to mouth.

He groaned with satisfaction, entwining our fingers as I deepened the kiss. Drew was a wildfire that burned fast and bright through my veins, consuming time and reason, with every brush of our lips feeding the flames. It didn't matter we'd just had sex and my hands had been all over him. The craving I knew for him was untamed, something that would never be defeated, only survived.

Only when the begging in my lungs turned to lightheadedness did I rip my mouth away for a few greedy breaths before dragging my burning lips across his stubble.

"I fucking love you," he rasped, dropping his forehead on my shoulder.

"I love you more," I whispered, kissing his uncombed hair before forcing myself away to gather up his clothes scattered around the gym.

"Okay, Captain One-up." His snarky comeback made me smile.

Dropping the clothes in a heap, I tugged the boxers free from his pants and handed them over. Once those were on, I handed him a shirt.

Seeing the fabric, he glanced up. "That's yours."

"Yours was on the floor."

"So?"

"So you can wear mine."

The dimple I fiercely loved indented his cheek, somehow making his blue eyes sparkle more. "You just want to be all over me."

I lifted an eyebrow. "You got a problem with that?"

He swiped the shirt and tugged it over his head. "Does it look like I have a problem with it?"

"It looks like you can't see," I teased, grabbing my comb to tackle the damp, wild mane.

After smoothing out the front, I gently nudged him around to tame the rest. Comfortable silence blanketed the room, the only sound an occasional drip from the shower.

Finished, I set aside the comb and wrapped around him from behind, rubbing my cheek against the side of his face.

Forever a slave to this man's scruff.

"You gonna tell me?" I asked.

An exhale moved through him, and he reached into his jeans to pull out his phone. After a few taps, he held it up so I could look at the illuminated photo.

The image was a punch to my midsection, momentarily robbing me of breath. A wave of love rolled through me, and I hugged Drew a little tighter.

Travis sat smiling behind the wheel of the Fastback, the morning sun streaming through the windshield igniting a flame of blue in his wind-whipped, coal-black hair. His eyes, just as dark as his hair, sparked with mischief. He looked weightless in that frozen moment. Free.

Trav was a lot of things. A good son and protective brother. He was smart, stubborn, fiercely loyal, and tended to be impulsive. There wasn't a single second of any day that I wasn't proud to be his dad.

But something he wasn't—at least not often—was free. The first five years of his life marked him. An unerasable tattoo on part of his core personality. And yeah, maybe like ink, it would fade with time, but it would always be permanent.

Sometimes it made me angry, knowing it didn't matter we'd had him for three times the amount of time his birth mother had, that we loved him infinitely more, but what she'd done would be ingrained in him forever.

It taught me that some scars can't be loved away. That truly loving someone meant loving the dark parts of them and understanding that sometimes no amount of light would ever penetrate that darkness.

And that I didn't need to erase that darkness but instead love it too.

"Mm," I hummed, still looking at the photo. "He's just like you. Happiest behind the wheel."

Drew lifted his face in my direction. "Not true, frat boy. I'm happiest with you."

"Sweet talker," I accused, enjoying the way my teeth ached from the sweetness.

"It's true."

I closed my lips around his ear and tugged. "I know, baby."

He fell quiet, gazing back at the photo.

"Just because he's just like you doesn't mean you are just like him."

"You always know," he whispered.

It was my job to know. To take care of him. Not just physically but emotionally. Taking the phone, I set it aside and then moved around to lower onto the closed toilet seat. I tugged his hand, and he came forward, straddling my thighs and surrendering his weight.

"If this toilet falls through the floor, you're explaining it to the fam."

"Ivy would just use it as an excuse to remodel the entire house."

Drew groaned. "She just did that last year."

"If we aren't ready, we aren't ready," I said, bringing it back before he tried to avoid the conversation more.

"He's ready." Drew's baby blues met mine, and the love he had for our son was right there on the surface. "God, T. He's a good driver. Gonna be better than me. I can feel it."

"Of course he is." I agreed, rubbing my palm up his spine. "Because you taught him."

Drew shook his head just once. "Some skills can't be taught. He's a natural. You can see how much he loves it."

"If we aren't ready. We aren't ready," I repeated.

"*We*." He scoffed. "You mean me."

I gripped his waist, emphasizing my words. "I mean *us*. Because if you aren't ready for Travis to have his own car, then I'm not either. We're a team."

"Aren't you scared?" he whispered.

My heart tumbled a little, as it always did when Drew showed his vulnerable side. It was a side I saw a lot more of after he'd nearly died. That accident changed us as a couple. The weakness it forced on us only made us stronger. And even though it had been many years, it didn't matter. Every time Drew was more openly dependent on me, more willing to show me that secret place he kept tucked behind his heart, something in me shattered and then quickly rebuilt so I could be stronger for him.

"Of course I am, baby," I murmured. Handing Trav the keys to his own car felt like a big deal. Not just in the regular sense of watching him drive off to school or knowing it was one step closer to him being an adult.

There was also a sense of worry because Trav could be impulsive and was a certified adrenaline junkie just like his father. At times, he had an explosive temper and carried a lot of deeply rooted anger. It was one of the reasons we encouraged him to play football because it was a good outlet. But football wasn't his passion. Cars were. And even though we basically lived and breathed fast cars, it was scary to hand our child a set of keys, especially after what we'd been through with Drew.

"But you think he's ready?"

"As ready as he can be," I replied. "You've made sure of it."

"What if it's not enough?" He worried.

It would be easy to say it was enough because Drew was always enough. But that wasn't reassuring, and it sounded contrived even if I did wholly mean it.

"Then we learn as we go. All of us. Together."

He nodded while tracing invisible patterns across my shoulder. "I'm afraid he's going to resent me. Think I'm holding him back."

"You aren't your father, Drew." I was firm. "You worrying about Trav's safety is not the same as your father refusing to let you chase your dreams to drive." *Or live any of the life you wanted.*

He exhaled. "I know. I'm just…"

Traumatized because your father is an asshat.

Drew had a lot of scars from how his father raised him under such rigid expectations and then later disowned him for loving me. And even though Drew permanently tossed his parents out of our lives twelve years ago—for damn good reason—he'd become haunted that he would somehow end up like his father and ruin his relationship with his son.

In my opinion, someone who loved like Drew could never alienate his own son, but I understood his fears. I'd rather pluck out my eyelashes with a pair of rusty pliers than invalidate any of Drew's worries with a lame "that will never happen."

"I have an idea."

"Does it involve whipped cream and naked time?"

I blinked.

Drew wagged his eyebrows.

I pursed my lips. "Who's the whipped cream for?"

Yeah, yeah, we were supposed to be talking seriously, but when my hot husband utters whipped cream and naked in the same sentence, consider me distracted.

A shit-eating grin transformed his face. "You don't know?"

"You shouldn't poke a horny bear, baby."

He leaned in to whisper, "I'd rather the horny bear poke me."

I growled and stood, lifting him as I went.

"Oh, what big muscles you have," he squealed.

I threw my head back and laughed. "Fuck off."

He laughed too, and soon, we ended up grinning at each other in the confines of the bathroom. The Adam's apple in his throat bobbed, and the humor in his eyes softened. "I wish we didn't have to go downstairs."

Pulling him against me, I nuzzled his cheek. "How about I take you out to dinner tonight? Just me and you. Some one-on-one time."

"Talk dirty to me, frat boy."

I smiled. "And maybe dessert will include that whipped cream you were talking about."

His arms slid around my neck. "You have really good ideas."

"That a yes?"

"That's a hell yes."

I kissed him quickly, then stepped back to finish dressing.

On the way downstairs, he tugged my hand. "T? What were you going to say back there?"

I told him, and the look on his face made my heart swell. Like I handed him the moon and stars and not just an idea.

"Our family is the moon and stars to me, T."

Confused, I met his stare. "You doing that mind-reading thing again?"

His teeth flashed, and the skin around his eyes wrinkled. "You're doing that talking out loud thing again."

"So you like the idea?"

"I more than like. This is exactly why I could never do parenting without you."

"You could," I refuted.

His head tilted, lips pursed. "But why would I want to?"

I smiled. "So green light?"

"Bright green. We can talk details at dinner tonight."

I scoffed. "We both know you will somehow have already found what you want online."

"What's online?" Ivy asked, stepping from behind the massive fridge door.

"If that fridge got any bigger, it would need its own zip code," Drew quipped.

Ivy lifted her palm. "I can't help it all the boys in this house eat more than some restaurants serve in an entire day."

"That's what happens when you shack up with a football player," Drew teased on his way to the coffee pot.

"You did the same thing," she pointed out.

"Guess we have good taste," he said, looking over his shoulder to wink at me.

Ivy passed me the creamer, and I carried it over to add some to Drew's mug.

"There you are!" Rimmel said, coming through the archway leading into the dining room. "We're almost out of pancakes, so you better go eat."

Dark wisps of hair that had come loose from her messy bun floated out around her head as she carried an empty bowl to the sink.

"The kids already demolished all the fruit," she informed just as her foot caught in the hem of her too-long pants and she pitched forward. The bowl went flying, hitting against the stone counter and splattering whatever was left.

I scooped her up before she could land in a heap, cradling her slight form in a bridal-style hold. She looked up at me, sheepish, hair in her face, and smudges on her glasses.

"I've come to accept that I'm never going to be graceful," she said, the tip of her nose pink.

I laughed. "It only took forty years to admit it, huh?"

She gasped. "How dare you, Trent? I am *not* forty!"

"Forty is one of them F-words," Braeden announced from the archway. "Just ask Drew. He knows. How's them old bones, bro?"

"You say that as if you aren't about to fall over the hill too," Drew muttered around his mug.

"Forty isn't old," I said. "It's just eighteen with twenty-two years of experience."

"I'm curious." B wondered. "Do you lie in bed at night and think up comebacks to defend your man?"

"I have better things to do in bed at night. I feel for Ivy if you don't know that."

The sound of coffee spewing followed by sputtering had me turning. Drew was coughing now, his eyes watering.

"You better get him a napkin," Rimmel said.

I walked over to the island and gestured for her to grab one since, you know, my arms were already full. Then I carried her over so she could hand it to Drew.

"That's my sister," he said, voice strained.

"Sisters before misters." I tossed out one of B's ancient lines.

Braeden appeared at my elbow. "Now see here. Your sister doesn't have any complaints."

"There are children present," Rimmel hissed.

B scoffed. "They're in the next room eating us out of house and home."

"No kid wants to hear about their parents' bedroom activity." Rimmel's nose wrinkled. "I don't want to hear about it either."

A tap on my shoulder had me turning.

Romeo looked between his wife and me, then raised his eyebrow.

"She almost killed herself," I explained. "It's safer this way."

"Are you causing trouble in here, smalls?"

"Me?" She gasped. "They're the ones talking about—" She paused to look around and then lowered her voice to a loud whisper. "*Sex.*"

Romeo's lips twitched, and he held out his arms. "Give me my wife."

"Thanks for the save, Trent."

I deposited her into Romeo's hold. "Anytime, sis."

Ivy picked up the bowl from the floor and tossed it into the sink. We stopped using glass a long time ago.

"I'm going to eat," I said, rubbing my grumbling stomach.

Drew grasped my hand on the way to the dinging room, and I smiled, tugging him along with me.

"Oh, for shit's sake!" Braeden hollered.

We glanced back to see him holding up his foot with a large wet spot covering his white sock.

"Tutor girl, one of your beasts pissed in the kitchen!"

Rimmel gasped. "They did not!"

"Then how do you explain this?" he exclaimed, jabbing at his foot.

"The stain is pink, moron. Obviously, it's not pee," Ivy pointed out and reached down to pull the sock off her husband's foot. Bravely, she lifted it to take a quick sniff, blond hair swaying with the motion. "It's watermelon juice," she told the room.

"*Ooops,*" Rimmel sang. Then, in a much louder voice, she called, "Milo! Rocket! Barney and Fred!"

There was a bark from somewhere, and then a horde of dogs stormed the kitchen, the excited click-clack of their nails on the floor just as loud as their panting breaths.

"Mess," Rimmel pointed to the spilled fruit juice, and the dogs nearly knocked Braeden over as they slurped it up with their massive tongues.

"This is unhygienic!" Braeden complained loudly. "These dogs are out of control."

Andi brushed through me and Drew and shot forward, her pin-straight dark hair blowing around her shoulders and a piece of bacon hanging from her fingers.

"Here, boy!" she called, waving it around.

Barney got there first, taking the entire thing in one chomp.

She laughed and raced back to the dining room, the dogs following her with hopeful looks. Across the kitchen, another dog burst in from the dog door and raced across the floor, sliding a bit as he ran. Seeing the sock dangling from Ivy's hand, he grabbed it and gave it a shake, then took off.

"That's my sock!" Braeden roared and lunged after the dog.

Rimmel giggled as Ketchup veered away and came over to hide behind Drew. When B tried to reach around him to get his beloved dog, Drew put a hand on his chest and shook his head.

"This is why he acts like that," B accused. "You let him get away with sock murder."

"It was ruined anyway," Drew said, reaching around to scratch Ketchup behind the ear. "Good boy," he whispered, and Ketchup's tail beat the back of my legs.

Yes, I know. I allowed him to name our dog Ketchup.

As previously mentioned, I am weak for him and anything that makes him happy. After our beloved French Fry crossed the rainbow bridge, we didn't think we'd want to get another pet. Death is hard. But then about a year later, Rimmel showed up with this guy who came into the shelter with matted hair and his ribs showing. The second he jumped into Drew's lap, I knew he was ours.

"This house is a damn zoo," Braeden mourned.

Romeo made a goat sound.

Rimmel and Ivy laughed.

"How could you do it to me, blondie?" Braeden accused.

Ivy made a sound and wrapped her arms around his neck. "Poor baby."

"Give me some sugar. I need it," he told her.

Drew made a sound and turned away. "I think I lost my appetite."

"Daddy!" Andi waved from down the table. "Sit by me," she said, slapping her hand on the seat of the empty chair beside her.

I caught Drew by the back of the neck and leaned in. "You sit. I'll make you a plate," I told him before brushing a kiss on his temple and nudging him toward our daughter.

Ketchup trailed after him, and I grabbed some plates and piled them high with pancakes, eggs, and bacon. There were also muffins and donuts, but I didn't just do all that work in the gym to undo it at the table.

I might not yet be forty like my husband, but I was no spring chicken either. It took a lot more discipline now to maintain my muscle than it did when I was twenty.

Maintaining it was important to me, not just for vanity either but because I wanted to be able to haul Drew around as long as he would let me. Andi too. Soon, she'd be twelve, and even though she was still a little peanut and easy for me to carry, I knew the day was approaching when she'd be "too old" for her dad to carry her around. I had to enjoy it while I could.

"Heads up, Uncle Trent!" Blue yelled, and I looked up in time to see a blob of scrambled egg coming at my face. I moved fast and ate it out of the air.

"Blue Jay Anderson, did you just throw eggs at your uncle?" Rimmel said, plunking her hands on her hips to glare at her son. At fourteen, he was taller than her.

"He looked hungry," Blue said. "You always did tell me to share." He smiled, and Rimmel's lips twitched.

Over her shoulder, she glared at Romeo. "This is your fault, Roman Anderson."

"Me? What did I do?"

She scowled. "Passing on that larger-than-life charm."

Romeo snatched her from behind and kissed her neck loudly.

All the kids groaned and gagged.

"But, baby, you like my charm," he reasoned.

"No more food throwing," Rimmel told the room.

Jax belched, and frankly, it was impressive.

"I felt the house shake!" Asher announced.

Blue and Jax high-fived.

"Ewww," Andi and London both sang.

"Boys are disgusting," Nova announced, not even looking up from her phone.

Ivy stopped behind her chair, a mug in her hand. "Oooh, that's cute," she said, pointing to something on the screen. "Send me the link."

"Done," Nova said a second later.

"Good, now put your phone down. It's family time."

Nova sighed. "Mom."

"You know the pancake Sunday rules," Braeden chimed as he sat at the table.

Rocket lumbered over and dropped his head on his lap. Braeden made a face but then scratched behind his ear.

Sucker.

After setting down our plates, I went and refilled Drew's coffee and added some creamer. On the way back to the table, I helped myself to a few sips before handing it back to him.

"Can I have some coffee?" Andi asked from beside Drew.

"It'll stunt your growth," he told her, then immediately took a long drink.

"Ha, her growth is already stunted," Travis quipped.

"Is not!" she hollered.

"I'm not the one who needs a stepstool to brush my teeth," he shot back.

"At least I brush my teeth, dragon breath!"

"*Oooh,* burn!" London jumped in.

"My growth's not stunted, is it, Daddy?" Andi said, lifting her big brown eyes to me.

My heart somersaulted just looking at that sweet face. I'd do anything for her. "'Course not, peanut. Why do you think I have to lift so many weights? I gotta have muscle to carry you around."

Trav opened his mouth, but I shot him a look. He rolled his eyes but closed his lips.

"If I'm so big, why do you call me peanut?" She wanted to know.

Plucking her out of her chair, I held her up, dangling her above my head. She laughed, her cheeks turning rosy while her long dark hair fell forward in a curtain around her face. "Because to me, you will *always* be my little peanut," I said, pulling her in to smack a kiss on her cheek. Instead of putting her back in the chair, I sat beside Drew with her on my lap.

"I really want to try coffee," Andi said, leaning over and batting her eyes at Drew.

He groaned, and I stifled a laugh.

"Fine. But just a small sip."

Andi clapped and sat up straight as though trying her dad's bean juice was a serious matter.

The mug was massive in her hands, the pink polish on her nails chipping and a small gold ring with a butterfly on it circling her index finger.

The intrauterine growth restriction she'd endured as a fetus due to her mother's heavy drug use resulted in an impairment in blood flow and also nutrition, causing her to be born prematurely and with a low birth weight. That, coupled with the poor nutrition and living conditions she was first introduced to, meant Andi was small in stature. Once adopted, she caught up quite a lot and no longer lacked in nutrients or vitamins. However, the doctors did think she would remain with a slight build, likely because of her early development and general genetics.

Slurping brought my attention back to the girl in my lap, and I smiled, watching her gulp down the coffee.

"I said a small sip, not half the mug," Drew told her.

I chuckled and took the mug from her hand. "Don't drink all of Daddy's coffee, peanut, or he will be grumpy."

Andi looked at me, lips glossy from the drink and a stoic look in her eyes. "It's not very good."

Everyone laughed.

"You don't like my coffee, peanut?" Drew asked, taking the mug back to help himself.

"It tastes burned."

"That's 'cause Uncle B made it," Romeo put in.

"I feel the love," B quipped.

"Your dad makes better coffee," Drew told her.

Andi looked at me, doubt written all over her face.

"Just stick to juice," I said, giving her a small glass of OJ.

She took it and then fed Ketchup a piece of bacon.

Drew handed me the mug, and I drank some before digging into my food.

"Next time you want to try coffee, Andi, I'll make you a latte," Nova offered.

"With caramel?" Andi asked.

"Sure."

Drew shook his head and grumbled about how the new generation couldn't appreciate real coffee.

"You're just mad you can't use the espresso machine," Ivy mused.

Rimmel laughed. "Last time he tried, frothed milk ended up everywhere but his cup."

"Who needs frothed milk anyway? That's what creamer is for," Drew said around a mouthful of pancake.

"How's the team looking for the new season?" Romeo asked Braeden.

Ever since a knee injury forced him into retirement from pro football, B had spent the last few years coaching his and Romeo's old high school team, the Green Hornets.

"Gonna be a helluva lot better with Blue and Jax playing this year," Braeden answered.

"Junior varsity," Blue said, a bit of remorse in his tone. He was just like Rome. Wanted to be the best, so he was already looking at varsity even though this would be his first year of high school.

"We all start somewhere." Romeo reminded him. "Junior varsity is just as important."

"It only matters if you have fun," Rimmel said.

"Junior varsity is where we need improvement. Varsity is looking solid. Right, Trav?"

"The quarterback isn't as good as Uncle Romeo."

Romeo let out a sound.

Braeden laughed.

"Not many are, son," I told him.

"That's why I'm glad we have you, Trav. To make sure no one mows him down before he gets the ball out."

Travis nodded, and I studied him a moment before turning back to the conversation.

"How about Alpha U, Rome? You nervous about your first season as head coach?"

"Nah. It only matters if we have fun," Romeo replied, tongue in cheek.

"Roman Anderson, are you making fun of me?"

He widened his blue eyes and smiled, very reminiscent of the way Blue did earlier. "I would never do that, smalls. You're my favorite."

She made a face.

Romeo slid her off her chair and into his lap. "It's gonna

be fun being back on campus. Like when we met," he said, resting his chin on her shoulder.

"I'll wear my hoodie to the games!" Rimmel said.

"That ratty old thing?" Braeden questioned. "You'll freeze to death."

Romeo pinched the fabric of his ancient Alpha U hoodie between two fingers and pulled it away from her arm. The blue was faded, the golden lettering half rubbed off, and there were probably at least a dozen holes in it.

"Maybe now that I'm back, I can get you a new one. One that says coach on the back," Romeo said.

"Fine, but you'll have to wear it at a few games before you give it to me."

"Deal," he whispered.

"What about you, Ives?" Drew asked, stealing some food off my plate because his was already empty. I pushed it toward him when he wasn't looking. I always added extra to my plate because he always ate off it.

"What's going on in the fashion world?"

"Fashion week is coming up in New York. I'm covering it for *People* but also for my own socials and website. LA Torres invited me backstage to help style a few models."

I wasn't sure who that was, but I knew enough to know he was probably some famous and exclusive designer.

"Can I please come?" Nova begged.

"You have school."

"It's LA Torres," Nova said as if that somehow explained it all.

Ivy pursed her lips. "It's your senior year."

"It's only a couple days. Please." Nova turned her baby blues on Braeden. Dude was fucked. That girl got her eyes from Drew (okay, technically Ivy), and they were irresistible. "Daddy, pleeease."

"You'll miss a game. Doesn't the squad need you?"

Nova was the cheer captain at the high school.

"Tayla can take over for one game."

Tayla was the co-captain.

All the best uncles keep up with the 4-1-1.

Braeden sighed.

"I'll bring you a brownie from that bakery you like." She sweetened the deal.

"What about me?" Romeo asked.

"You too, Uncle Romeo."

"Fine." B relented. "But only if you take a bodyguard."

"Braeden," Ivy admonished.

Excitement shone in Nova's eyes, and when she shot up from the table, her long dark hair (which she got from her father) floated around and stuck to Braeden's unshaven jaw when she hugged him. "Thank you, Dad! I love you."

Braeden grunted. "Two bodyguards."

Ivy tossed up her hands. "Anyone else want to come?"

"Me!" London and Andi exclaimed.

"You girls can come when you're older," Ivy promised.

"Don't playoffs begin in the NRR soon?"

"In about two weeks," Drew answered. "Perks of not being in NASCAR. Those suckers don't get any break between end of season and start of playoffs like we do."

"Fall is coming at us fast and furious like always," Rim concluded.

"Yeah, but this time I'll be home for all of it," Romeo said.

"But before summer is officially over, we have one more thing to celebrate," I said, glancing down the table at Travis.

"Trav's birthday party is gonna be lit," Asher announced.

Everyone laughed.

"No one says lit anymore," Nova told him.

"Have you been on that clock app again?" Rimmel asked. We were all very strict about social media in this house. We had to be. The paparazzi had never been kind.

"Yeah, on Nova's phone," Asher said, making a face at Nova.

"What are you doing with that app?" Ivy wanted to know.

"Everyone has it, Mom!" Nova defended herself. Then to Asher, she added, "As if I'd tell you the passcode to my phone."

"Don't need it when you have face ID. I'm surprised it even recognized you with the way you were drooling." Asher leaned back in his seat and feigned sleep with his mouth hanging open and started to snore.

"I do not look like that!" she demanded.

"You totally do." Jax snickered.

Jax, Blue, and Asher laughed.

Nova pushed back from the table and stood. "I'm going to my room."

"We aren't done with breakfast," Ivy said.

"I am," Nova said.

"You can go to your room when we're done," Braeden said, no give in his voice. "Sit."

With a huff, Nova sat back down.

"Boys, apologize to your sister," Romeo said.

"She's not my sister," Asher argued.

"What did you just say?" Romeo's voice was even and quiet.

All the kids straightened.

Asher spoke up first. "Sorry for making fun of your sleep face, Nova."

Drew glanced at me, and I bit back a laugh.

"Sorry for agreeing with him," Jax said.

"Same." Blue agreed.

Romeo looked at Blue.

Blue sighed. "Sorry, Nova."

"Now, about Travis's birthday party," Ivy said. She was forever the event planner of this family. "I double-checked yesterday with the caterer to make sure everything was confirmed. We are good to go for Saturday."

Nova perked up. "Saturday? *This* Saturday?"

"His birthday is the same every year. It's kind of an annual thing," Jax told her.

"Obviously," Nova quipped. "I guess I just thought it was next Saturday."

"Did you make plans for this Saturday?" Ivy asked.

Nova bit down on her lip.

"What's wrong, honey?" Rimmel pressed.

"Well..." She began, glancing down at her lap. "It's just... I have a date."

A beat of silence rippled across the table. Then Ivy reacted. "A date! Your first date."

Braeden's fork clattered against the plate.

Here we go.

"Braeden," Ivy warned.

He was stone silent as he swiped his mouth with a napkin, the picture of etiquette. A fault line about to snap from pressure. After tossing the napkin down, he said, "I think I must have heard wrong. Critter, can you say that again?"

Nova looked at Ivy who nodded reluctantly.

"Jordan Falls asked me to the movies."

Braeden erupted, his chair shooting back as he bolted upright. "That putz! Oh, hells no!" he hollered.

Ivy and Rimmel gasped in unison. "Braeden!"

Braeden shook his head adamantly. "No way is my baby girl going out with one of my football players."

"But, Dad!"

"Don't *dad* me. Hells no." He exhaled, pushing a hand through his hair. "Jordan Falls." He scoffed. Turning to Romeo, he said, "Kid's last name is an omen. He trips on his cleats more than he catches a ball."

"Dad! I like him. I've been waiting forever for him to ask me out."

"Shoulda cut him from the team," B grumbled.

I rolled my lips in to keep from laughing and looked at Romeo who was doing the same.

Our daughters weren't old enough to date. Thank fuck.

"That's enough, Braeden. You're being ridiculous," Ivy said, standing up to face him. She was taller than Rimmel but still short compared to Braeden.

She didn't care, though. She faced off with that dude on the regular.

Always won too.

"It's a date, not a marriage proposal."

Braeden made a choked sound. "Football players are pervs, baby. She can go out with someone who plays chess."

Drew, Rome, and I burst out laughing. Most of the kids did too.

"Braeden James, are you calling my sons and my nephews perverts?" Rimmel demanded.

He blanched and looked at all our football player sons sitting around the table. "Present company excluded."

Rim snorted.

Nova wailed. "I'm going into senior year, and I haven't even been on a date. Do you know how embarrassing that is? No one wants to date me!"

"That isn't true," Ivy insisted. "Any boy would be lucky to spend time with you."

"I didn't even have a date to the winter formal last year." She went on. "I must be ugly."

Ivy and Rimmel gasped. "You are not ugly!"

"Look at what you've done, Braeden," Ivy accused.

"Me?" He defended himself. "I'm just saying he ain't good enough."

Nova started crying.

Jax sighed. "Everyone thinks you're hot."

"What?" Nova asked.

Jax rolled his eyes. "It's all I hear. *Dude, your sister is so hot. Dude, can I get your sister's number?*"

Beside him, Blue nodded emphatically as though he'd heard it all too.

Nova sniffled. "Really?"

"You better not be handing out your sister's number," Braeden deadpanned. "What are these boys doing going around looking at girls for? They're supposed to be at school to learn."

Romeo heckled. "Is that what you did in school, B? *Learn.*"

"Your time is coming, Rome," Braeden snapped.

That shut him up.

"They're scared to ask you out." Travis spoke up.

Nova's blue eyes shot to him. "What?"

"Your dad is the football coach, and he played for the NFL. Your uncle is Romeo Anderson. They're all afraid to ask."

"Should be," B declared.

Romeo nodded.

"Dad, you're ruining my life!" Nova announced. Then. "You too, Uncle Romeo."

Braeden and Romeo looked proud of themselves.

"Are boys going to be scared to ask me out too?" London asked.

Romeo shot up, his chair flying just like Braeden's did. "You're twelve years old!"

"I was just asking, Daddy," she said innocently, a mini version of her mother staring up at him with wide blue eyes behind a pair of glasses with purple frames.

Romeo made a choked sound and lowered beside her chair. After smoothing some of her long dark hair away from her face, he pushed the glasses up on her nose. "You don't need to worry about boys, strawberry. Daddy will take care of you."

"Can we get a puppy?"

"Hells no," Braeden replied.

"Sure, baby." Romeo agreed.

"*Rome*." Braeden was plaintive. "We already have fifteen dogs up in here."

"We do not," Rimmel declared. "We only have six right now, and two of them go to practices with you every day. And Ketchup is Drew's!"

Romeo glanced over his shoulder. "It's better than a boy."

B pursed his lips and glanced at Nova. "You want a puppy too?"

"This is ridiculous," Rimmel said.

Romeo turned to her. "You want to get a puppy, smalls?"

Rimmel melted. "I was thinking about bringing home that Aussie mix. He's been at the shelter for two weeks. No one's adopted him."

"We can go get him later today," Romeo promised.

Dude was one thousand percent wrapped.

"Can't you tell them my dads aren't that scary?" Nova asked Travis.

Her dads. No one even batted an eye. Romeo was practically her second dad. Drew and me too.

Travis shrugged a shoulder. "I could."

Nova leaned forward. "Then why haven't you?"

A brief dark look crossed Trav's face. "Because Uncle Braeden is right. They're not good enough."

Drew and I shared a look.

"You threatened them too!" Nova burst out.

"I don't threaten," Travis replied.

"Travis," I said quietly.

He glanced at me. "I didn't."

I conceded because I saw the truth in his stare. The thing

with Trav was that he didn't have to threaten. People instinctively knew not to mess with him. Apparently, people also knew that extended to his sisters.

"Mom!" Nova roared.

"All right, that's enough. Obviously, you can't go out on Saturday."

"But, Mom—"

"It's Travis's birthday. Family first. So you will have to go out on a different night. If Jordan doesn't understand that, then he's not worth your time."

"Why don't you just invite him to the party?" Rimmel suggested.

Braeden let out a wounded sound, laying his hand on his heart. "BBFL betrayal. How could you, sis?"

"That is a good idea." Ivy seconded.

"It's like they pretend I'm not even here," Braeden put in.

I finished off my plate of food. Frankly, this breakfast was like dinner and a show.

"You'd really let him onto the compound?" Nova asked.

We didn't let many people onto our family compound, mostly just family and a few friends of the kids who had been around for many years. We liked to keep this place private—a safe space for the family to be themselves. We'd had too many run-ins with the press and people selling information about us. It seemed like every time we stepped out in public, there was a camera somewhere. It was hard on the kids at first because they couldn't just have people over whenever they wanted. All their playdates were off the compound. Sometimes they still got mad about it, but we held our ground because you didn't realize how important safety and privacy were until they were taken away.

"It would be a great chance for us to meet him," she said, glancing at Braeden.

"And then after the party, you can go to the movies," Ivy added.

"He's not going to want to come here." She glanced at me and Drew. "Not with all my dads here."

"Well, he was brave enough to ask you out. He must really like you." Ivy encouraged her.

Nova said, "You think so?"

"One way to find out."

Nova turned to Travis. "Is it okay if I invite Jordan to your party?"

Travis shrugged. "Whatever."

"Travis," Drew admonished.

Travis sighed. "Sure, Nova. It's cool."

Nova got up and rushed around the table to throw her arms around his shoulders and hug him. "Thanks, Trav. I'm going to go text him," she called, running out of the room.

"Where's my hug?" Braeden yelled after her.

"Later!" she yelled back.

"Do you think he will come?" Rimmel asked.

"I hope not," Braeden grumbled. "How'd she get his number anyway? Better not have got it off my roster. Gonna have to start locking it up."

"If he comes, his phone stays at the door," Romeo said, and we all nodded.

"Can we go play Xbox now?" Asher asked.

"Put your dishes in the sink," Rimmel said.

Asher, Blue, and Jax all stood to gather their plates.

"You coming?" Blue asked Travis.

"Yeah," he replied and stood.

"Hey," Drew said, and Travis looked up from gathering his dishes.

"Me and your dad are going to dinner tonight. Can you hang with Andi?"

"Sure."

Drew swallowed. "If you want, you can take her out for ice cream."

Our son's face snapped up in surprise. "Really?"

"Ice cream!" Andi started bouncing around in her chair. "I want to get chocolate peanut butter with chocolate sprinkles."

"My girl knows how to eat," Braeden said.

"Extra sprinkles!" she declared.

"For real?" Travis pressed, looking between Drew and me.

"You have to take the SUV," I warned. If he was driving his sister around, there would be no Mustang.

He nodded. "Sure."

"Just ice cream and straight home," Drew added.

Travis nodded.

"Can I come too?" London asked.

"Ahhh," I faltered, brain scrambling for a way to say no. Before I could come up with something, Romeo spoke up. "As long as Travis says it's okay."

I glanced at Romeo, surprised. He was already looking at me like he was waiting. The second our eyes connected, he nodded once and then turned back to my son.

Travis nodded. "Sure, Lo. You can come too."

Andi and London beamed. Two peas in a pod.

"I'll get sprinkles too, Uncle B."

He tapped his heart and then pointed at London, making her giggle.

"Ice cream and a puppy!" London exclaimed as she and Andi grabbed their plates and headed into the kitchen. "This is the best pancake Sunday ever."

Braeden groaned.

"I can really take them to get ice cream. By myself?" Travis asked, looking at Drew.

Drew nodded. "Yeah. We trust you. Just drive safely, okay?"

"I promise."

When all the kids were gone, I glanced across the table at Romeo. "You know it's the first time we're letting him drive Andi somewhere without us."

"He's had his license for a while now," Rimmel said.

"He's a good driver. Drew taught him well," Ivy added.

Romeo met my eyes, then Drew's. "We trust him."

Everyone started cleaning up the dining room, but I laid my palm on Drew's thigh before he could get up.

"I'm proud of you, baby. So fucking proud."

"It's just ice cream, T."

Gently grasping his chin, I pulled him around so I could look in his eyes. "I'm proud of you."

His eyes softened, and he nodded.

Because we both knew it wasn't just ice cream. It was a start.

3

Drew

Trent might have been the one to ask me out on a date, but I was the one driving.

Duh.

"So where we going, frat boy?" I asked from the driver's seat of my sweet Fastback. She was proof that some things got even better with age.

Well, T was solid proof of that too, sprawled out in the passenger seat, taking up every inch of space with his thick jean-clad thighs and well-toned chest wrapped in a T-shirt he stole from my side of the closet.

It looked better on him, molded around his biceps and broad shoulders, a worn-out image of some fries across his torso.

The band on his finger had been there since the moment I'd put it there, and the leather strap of his watch was worn. He had not one gray hair to speak of, the dirty bastard. It seemed I'd gotten my *and* his share. His sandy hair was a little long on the top, and the way he ran his hands through it made it part to the side and fall over his forehead.

"I was thinking that new French bistro across town. I know you're anxious to try out the escargot," he said, not even able to try and con me with a straight face.

I shook my head and sighed. "You finally take me out on a date after months, and I get snails? Being old and married has changed you."

Laughing, he leaned over the console to invade my personal space. "I called over to Ernie's. He's holding the back booth."

A smile split my face. "Now you're talking."

"Only the best for you, babe," he mused, withdrawing to the other side.

I caught the front of his shirt and tugged him back. "If you want me to drive, you gotta give me some gas."

His mouth covered mine without hesitation, hand wrapping around the back of my head to hold me in place while his tongue bulldozed mine. I groaned into the kiss, getting swept away by the pull between us.

T started to pull away too soon, but I tightened the fist in his shirt and made a sound, and he came back enthusiastically, our teeth colliding with the effort. He chuckled, and I bit down on his lower lip, making his nostrils flare. My stomach buzzed with desire as I chewed lightly on his lower lip, tugging it away from his face before releasing it.

"Forget dinner," Trent said, reaching for me again.

I smacked his hand away and started the engine, its rumble filling the air.

"Fries before guys."

He collapsed back into his seat with a laugh.

"I'll drive. You shift."

His head rolled across the seat toward me, a lazy grin tugging the corners of his mouth.

He was enough to make a man forgo fries.

"Let's do it." He agreed, dropping his hand on the gearstick.

I drove way too fast and maybe blew a stop sign on the way to Ernie's Diner, a place we'd been coming to since before we even admitted we could never just be friends.

You know what they say: *The more things change, the more they stay the same.* And French fries at Ernie's with my guy was something that would never change.

The neon red of the diner sign reflected off the windshield when I pulled in to park. The scent of grease and pancakes filled my nostrils the second I flung open the door and got out. I breathed deep, appreciating the nostalgia this place always made me feel.

"Ahh, nothing like the smell of clogged arteries and asphalt," I mused, slamming the door behind me.

Trent's sneakers squeaked when he vaulted over the hood of the Fastback and landed by the front tire, a few pieces of loose gravel skittering as he straightened. "I am not getting any younger," he mused, putting a hand to his back like some oldie.

"Well, I think you're sexy as hell," I said, stepping up so close that the toes of our sneakers knocked.

"Yeah?" he asked, his voice low and rumbly. Sexy as hell.

I nodded. "Uh-huh."

Gaze darkening, he slid his hands into my open leather jacket to palm the sides of my waist. The battle the sun put up for summer lost the second it dipped below the horizon, and autumn stole the night, leaves rustling against the moody backdrop of darkness and filling the air with its sharp bite.

"Kiss me like you mean it."

I didn't have to, but I pushed onto my toes and wrapped my arms around his neck, my elbows bending at how close I pushed. Instead of going in for the kiss immediately, I glanced up to the sky and dragged my chin across his lips, tickling them with my scruff.

He groaned deep in his throat, and I smiled, doing it again because this man was such a sucker for my beard and I loved riling him up. The pads of my fingers grazed the back of his jaw, and his warm breath whispered across my skin.

"Mask," he warned in that sexy-as-fuck tone.

The second I lowered my chin, he was on me, lips like Velcro affixing themselves to mine and gripping like they would never let go. I melted against him, loving the way his muscles locked up to support mine while his tongue did a thorough search of my mouth.

There wasn't a place inside me this man hadn't found, but he was never complacent, always searching, always willing to take on more.

I loved him so intensely some days it felt like my heart beat just for him. It didn't matter how much love I gave to everyone else. I always had more because the reason my heart knew love at all was him.

His hands slipped around to the small of my back, pulling me closer, and I rubbed against him, the scent of his familiar cologne mixing with the leather of my jacket and—

Beeeeeeeep!

Our lips popped apart when I jolted back, the air slapping against my damp lips and making me shiver.

"I got you," Trent murmured, not even shaken by the loud interruption.

"Get a room!" someone yelled.

Trent stuck his arm in the air, his middle finger on clear display as his free hand palmed the back of my head and pulled me back in.

The warmth of his lips made me sigh, and I kissed him again while he held the rest of the world at bay.

When he was done, he pulled back slowly, dropping two final kisses before lifting his head. Mind fuzzy, I blinked as the sounds and scents of night came back.

"How about those fries?"

The urge to snuggle into his chest and beg to be held was right there on my tongue, the craving suddenly stronger than fries. But this was date night, so I held out my hand and let him lead me inside.

You know what I'd learned since waking up from a coma?

Since my life was irrevocably changed and I became a husband and a father?

Giving up control to someone else once in a while didn't make me weak like I thought it would for so long. It was just the opposite. It made me stronger.

The radio was playing oldies, and it competed with the busy line cook flipping burgers and chopping hashbrowns while the dishwasher clinked dishes and tossed silverware around.

A few booths were full and there were people at the counter eating pie, but Trent didn't let go of my hand, just walked confidently toward the back of the bullet, our arms stretching between us as I followed.

When we got to the booth in the back, he smiled and picked up a piece of wide-ruled notebook paper with the word *reserved* scrawled across in black pen.

"Thanks, Ernie!" Trent called, waving the paper toward the counter.

I had no idea if that was even the guy's name or if it came with the place when he bought it, but we always called him that and he always answered. Today, his answer was a whistle followed by laughter.

Trent turned to me and winked. "Only the best for you, baby."

Snickering, I slid into the faux-leather booth beside him,

pushing right up against his side. He draped his arm around my shoulders and kicked his feet onto the seat on the other side of the table.

"Remember when you used to sit across from me?" he said, pointing with the hand draped over my chest.

"That's too far now," I replied, settling deeper into him.

"It was too far then too."

I laid my head on his shoulder, both of us ignoring the menu. We'd been here so many times over the years that I could probably recite it in my sleep.

A waitress dressed in jeans, a red T-shirt, and a black waist apron strode down the aisle between booths and slid a large red basket lined with checkered paper loaded down with golden fries in front of us.

A sound of appreciation ripped right out of me as I straightened and dug in. The hot fry was crisp on the outside and softer inside with the salt melting on my tongue with a zing.

So good. "Have I died and gone to heaven?" I wondered and shoved another three in my mouth.

She laughed and shook her head. "Aren't you going to share?"

"No. I need ketchup, frat boy."

"Who says romance is dead?" Trent mused, already dumping a puddle of the good stuff into the basket.

"You boys having your usual?" the waitress asked.

"That would be great," T replied while I nodded around a mouthful.

She returned a few moments later with two glasses with tiny bubbles fizzing to the surface and crowding the ice. What was left of the foamy head crackled, condensation already forming on the outside, hinting at the chill within.

I abandoned my fries long enough to grab a straw, rip the paper off the end, and blow the rest of it at my husband.

Laughter shook his body, and he plucked it off his chest to tie a knot in the center and drop it on the table beside my fries.

Ah, good times.

Satisfied with our little tradition, I grabbed another golden stick of happiness, swirled it in ketchup, and held it out to my guy.

He arched an eyebrow. "You're sharing?"

"It's getting cold."

The corner of his mouth lifted, and he leaned forward, lips parting.

I yanked it back and shoved the entire thing in my mouth. "Too slow."

"Greedy bastard," he mused fondly.

Salty fingers smudged his jeans when I laid my palm on his thigh and squeezed. "I am," I concurred quietly. "Greedy for all the things I love most."

"That include me?"

"Oh, you're at the top of the list."

My skin prickled when his lips brushed my ear, and the hair on the back of my neck stood when he whispered, "That mean you're going to eat me later too?"

"I've always got room for you."

"Order's up!" Our waitress returned carrying two plates piled with food. A cheeseburger and fries for me—*yes, more fries*—and a Reuben on rye with fries for T.

"This looks great. Thank you," T said, tugging his plate closer.

"You boys need anything else?"

"We're good," Trent replied as I flipped the bun off the top of my burger and grabbed the thick slices of tomato.

T lifted the bread on his sandwich, and I laid them on his beef and then uncapped the bottle of Heinz to pour a big puddle on his plate and then on mine.

I helped myself to his fries and ketchup, sighing appreciatively.

I reached for my soda, but Trent made a sound, freezing my arm midair. "You're gonna get ketchup all over your sleeve," he scolded, abandoning his plate to tug the leather jacket down so it wasn't dragging in the food.

We ate in comfortable silence for a few after that. The burger oozed the perfect amount of grease and the fries on T's plate the perfect amount of salt.

After swiping my burger through the ketchup, I pointed to the near-empty spot. "You're almost out."

"You still have some," he mused, motioning to the untouched mound on my plate.

"It's not the same."

He shook his head but added more to his plate.

"You think the kids are okay?" I asked.

T pulled out his phone and brought up the app we had to track their whereabouts. "They're at Sweetstone," he said, turning the device around to show me the map. "Andi is probably covered in chocolate."

I pulled out my cell and brought up the tab I still had open from earlier and set it beside his plate. Trent leaned forward to gaze at the screen and then picked up the phone to look closer.

When he looked up, his eyes glimmered with amusement. "How long have you had this picked out?"

"I saw the listing a couple weeks ago. Didn't think too much of it, but then today when you suggested getting Trav a car that needed work, it came to mind."

Trent scrolled through the listing, squinting a bit to read it.

"You need glasses."

"I do not."

"Do too," I sang.

"These words in this listing are just small," he argued.

"I think you in a pair of glasses would be sexy as hell."

His hazel eyes fired up. "You think?"

"Mmhmm." I agreed. "Just thinking about it makes me hard."

Trent's stare dropped to my lap, then back up. "Maybe glasses wouldn't be so bad."

Smirking, I stole the last few fries off his plate, then washed them down with the perfectly carbonated soda.

"It's a Mach 1 like mine, but the '70 has a different styling and trim," I said, bringing the conversation back to the car. "This one has two headlights instead of four and a cleaner front design. The fender lights are replaced with air scoops."

"They're missing," Trent noted.

I nodded. "Yeah, we'll have to fix that. The side markers are more rectangular on this one versus mine."

Still thumbing through the listing, Trent said, "It needs a new engine, tires, probably lights. Needs a sway bar kit and coilover suspension for better cornering. It doesn't say, but I'm guessing it will need a new fuel injection too for better drivability."

"I love it when you talk dirty to me."

Trent laughed. "Trav would definitely love the black. Personally, I think some red trim would be sick, but that would be up to him."

Adrenaline was already pumping through my veins. Just the idea of getting this car into our garage and being under the hood with our son was pumping me up. "You like it?"

"Baby, you could show me a tricycle with two missing wheels, and I would agree just for the look on your face alone."

"Frat boy," I whined, half amused and half frustrated. "I want your honest opinion."

"I think we should go look at it. I also think the seller is on crack if he thinks he's getting what he's listed it for. Not with all the upgrades it's gonna need."

God, he was fucking hot. He was also really good with numbers and negotiations.

Like *really* good.

"I totally understand why Romeo got so hot over a nerd. You really need to get those glasses."

His crooked front tooth flashed, and I thought about climbing into his lap right there. I was saved from embarrassing myself when he continued talking.

"This is gonna be six months of work, easy. Probably closer to eight."

I nodded. "Probably."

His knowing eyes met mine. "That would give you plenty of time to get used to Trav with his own car."

"Would give both of us time to spend with him while we help him build it."

"Call and set it up," T said, setting aside the phone.

"You know if we buy him this car, it will only be a matter of time before he starts racing," I warned.

Leaning in, T hooked his palm around the back of my neck. The touch was grounding and reassuring, as was the tilt of his head to meet my eyes. "You okay with that?"

He was the picture of patience as I thought it over and nodded.

T gave my neck a squeeze before pulling back. "Good thing I have a lot of practice loving an adrenaline junkie."

The loss of his touch accompanied by his words made me feel like an engine about to sputter out. "T..." My voice was gruff, slightly pained.

He came back immediately, the heavy weight of his hand pure relief. I slumped a little, breath puffing out. "Better?" he asked low.

I nodded.

"What is it, Drew?"

I wrinkled my nose.

"Baby." He modified.

Better.

"I think I want to retire." The words whooshed out of me like a blown tire. Fast, forceful, and shocking.

His fingertips jerked against my neck before tightening with his intake of breath. "What?"

Body twisting toward him, I lifted my leg so my bent knee was resting on his, my upper body swaying closer. His hand wedged between my bent knee and tugged me closer while he rotated his upper half to face mine.

The hand not against my neck dove inside my jacket to grip my waist.

"I've been thinking about it for a while now, T. I think it's time."

"I knew there was something," he murmured almost to himself.

"What?"

"I knew there was something more than Travis pushing for a car and nearing graduation. I *knew*," he swore softly. "I didn't want to push. Should I have pushed?"

"Nah. I had to get to this particular finish line on my own."

His hand moved, cupping the side of my head instead of my neck. His eyes never settled, the hazel flickering between gold, green, and a stormy color in between. I realized then why, over the years, I'd stopped loving summer in favor of fall... because autumn was right there in his eyes.

"You're *never* on your own." The quiet vehemence in his words soothed the frayed edges of my nerves.

The corner of my mouth tilted up. "I know."

"If you're ready to talk, I'm ready to listen."

I was. But not here. "Wanna go parking?"

Molten honey flashed in his gaze. "Hells yes, I do."

I tapped his thigh, and we made a mad dash for the door, with T stopping long enough to put a pile of cash on the counter. "Keep the change!" he called.

Outside, I tossed him the keys, and he caught them, surprise flashing on his face. "You don't want to drive?"

"Will you?"

He nodded, unable to hide the worry on his face.

Closing the space between us, I grabbed his shirt, tugging at the hem. "I'm fine, frat boy. I just plan to be too busy to drive."

Lust made his lashes droop, but then he recovered. "I thought you wanted to talk."

"I do. But I need a little encouragement first."

"Get in the car," he growled, pushing me toward the Mustang.

We weren't even out of the parking lot before I was leaning over the console and reaching for the button on his jeans. He cursed low, and a smug, possessive feeling tightened my chest.

The faint sound of the fly sliding down made me anxious, and I quickly pushed under his boxers to wrap my hand around his aroused dick.

He took a turn a little too sharp, and my body fell farther into his lap, so I dipped my head for a mouthful of man and cotton all at once.

Trent's body sang, thighs flexing under me as I shoved the clothing away to get my lips fully around him. The thick weight was just what I needed, and I swallowed around him while flattening my tongue along the underside of his shaft.

Fingertips brushed my hair, and he whispered my name. Eyes sliding closed, I listened to the rumble of the engine and breathed deep the concentrated scent of my husband while nuzzling my nose in his coarse hair.

His dick spasmed, growing even thicker and stretching my lips. I slicked him up, sliding up and down his shaft before giving in to temptation and sinking to hold him inside me. A sound of satisfaction rumbled my throat, and T scratched against my scalp.

"There you go, baby," he murmured. "Just relax."

My body ached from being stretched across the console, torso twisted at an odd angle so I could stuff my face into his lap. I didn't care about any of it. All I cared about was having Trent inside me, tasting him with every swallow.

Trent was the master of a blow job. Getting head from him was second to none. But there was also something about holding him in my mouth. The constant warm pressure against my tongue and the way he pulsed every so often was reassuring. It was a quiet, close connection that helped soothe a lot of the anxiety I had from PTSD after my accident and then again when I returned to driving. We didn't do this as often as we used to, but sometimes when there was something big on my mind, this helped quiet the world so I could think.

Plus, it was a hell of a lot cheaper than therapy.

Years ago, I never would have allowed myself to ask for this. Hell, I probably wouldn't even have given myself a chance to realize this was something I loved. But intimacy took on a whole new level for us after I almost died. I would never be anywhere safer than with Trent.

His arm moved when he downshifted, brushing against my leather jacket. Instead of pulling back, he draped it over me, and I sighed into his skin.

I kept his cock warm as he drove over back roads I knew so well that I didn't even have to look up to know where we were. We were almost to a place we sometimes parked when T's jeans started vibrating right beside my face.

I grunted at the intrusion but made no move whatsoever to fish the ringing phone out of his pocket.

Go away.

His arm lifted, and I wrinkled my nose. "It's Travis," he said after glancing at the smartwatch around his wrist.

I pulled off and watched his hips lift so he could grab his phone. Before answering, he glanced at me and laughed under his breath. "You look drunk."

"I like your dick."

"Come back over here and get it."

I glanced at the phone lit up with Trav's name. "Our son is calling."

"I won't tell if you won't."

What a perv.

I must really like pervs, though, because I dove back into his lap as though I were starved.

My lips were sliding down over him when he accepted the call.

"Hey, Trav."

A few moments later, T's body went rigid beneath me. "What?"

I paused and strained to listen but couldn't make out what he was saying.

If Trent was rigid before, he was now stone. His entire frame coiled with tension that no man could withstand for long. "Where are you?" he demanded. His low swears filled the interior of the fastback. "Put her on," he said, gruff.

I sat up, mouth dry and eyes wide at his thunderous expression and tight grip on the steering wheel.

The second Andi came on the line, he exhaled as if trying to bring his level of rage down to something manageable. "Hey, peanut," he said, voice much softer than everything else about him. "What's going on?"

I heard the sound of our daughter's voice over the line,

not hearing her words but understanding immediately that something was wrong.

"T," I said, worry shattering my mellow mood.

He made a sound. "Okay, baby girl. We're coming home right now." Pause. "Promise. I'm coming right now."

She said something else. *Is she crying?*

Oh, hells no.

"I love you too, peanut. Now put your brother back on," Trent said gently. As soon as Travis was on the line, Trent's tone changed, hinting at the anger and worry he felt. "Is London with you?"

Trav spoke.

"Put her on."

A second later, Trent's voice went soft again. "Lolo, are you okay?"

London must have said she was because Trent nodded. "Good. That's good. Do you want me to call your dad?"

At those words, I rushed to pull my phone from my jacket to check the screen. There were no missed texts or calls, which was good, but I pulled up Romeo's number just in case.

It took everything in me not to shout for an explanation, but I wouldn't, not while T was talking to the kids.

"All right. Well, we are on our way now, okay?"

"Travis," he said the second our son was back on the line. "How are you?"

I didn't blame the kids for calling T first. I would have done the same thing. The man was a rock. Not just a rock but a force field. An entire barrier of fierce energy that made not just me feel protected but our kids too.

"I know, son. It's okay." He went on, his voice reassuring. "You did good. Are you okay to drive?"

My heart rate spiked, and pungent fear slammed into my chest. "Trent."

"You sure?" he asked, then nodded. "Okay. Meet you there. Be careful. If anyone follows you, drive straight to the police station."

My hand slapped onto his arm and squeezed. "*Trent.*"

He ended the call and dropped the phone into his lap before performing a sharp U-turn right there in the middle of the road. The engine responded beautifully as he shot forward in the opposite direction.

"What in the ever-loving fuck is wrong with people?" he spat, pushing the Mustang harder with his wrath.

I wanted to demand an explanation. I wanted all the information. But my heart was in my throat, panic swelling my tongue.

"It's one thing to send bullshit letters, but approaching a child in public?"

Ice formed in my veins. "*What*?"

His face whipped in my direction, realization dawning. He lifted a hand to wrap it around mine and squeeze. "They're fine." He assured me. "There wasn't an accident. They're fine."

"Then why was Andi crying?" I demanded. "Where are they?"

"They're on the way home from the ice cream place. Trav pulled over after he got them out of there because Andi was so upset."

He glanced at me from the corner of his eye, and I braced myself.

I blew out a long exhale. "Is this about those goddamn letters?"

Trent's lips rolled in and then popped open. "Yeah."

Here's the thing. There is no bracing yourself for fuckery involving your children. There never was and there never would be. Kids were off-limits. Full stop.

But here's the other thing… Some people had no limits.

Some people would do anything for a payday. Including hurting my baby girl.

"Oh, hells no," I roared.

The rage. *The fucking rage* that swept through me was unmatched. It burst in my center with so much intensity that it hit my fingers and toes in record time. The tips of my ears burned, and I fought past the whooshing sound filling my head to turn to Trent.

Trent didn't try and calm me. There was no calming down a father whose children were being threatened.

"Apparently, she tried to take her. Told Andi she never gave her up and we just took her."

Black spots swam in my vision. "I will kill them."

"Not if I get there first."

"Now's not the time for your one-upping, Trent," I snapped.

"I'm serious."

A heavy hush suffused the interior of the car. His words lacked the poison I used to spew mine, and somehow it made the threat much more lethal. T was an even-tempered guy, laid-back and watchful.

But God help the soul who evoked his anger.

It was so powerful that it made mine feel manageable.

Turning to him, I asked, "How is Andi?"

His tongue slid over his teeth. "She was crying."

I nodded. "Travis?"

"Shaken but holding it together because he's with the girls."

"He gets that from you," I murmured.

T shot me a look. "What?"

"His strength."

"He had that before we got to them," Trent said quietly. "It's why Andi is alive." The muscle in Trent's jaw flexed. "He shouldn't have to be strong. Not about this."

"*Fuck.*" I stared out the windshield, watching the pavement roll by as the headlights illuminated the road home. Trent was doing at least thirty over the speed limit, and when we turned onto one of the main roads, he barely slowed down.

By now, everyone around here knew this car. They knew who it belonged to and where we lived. I wondered how fast the cops would show up, and the thought spurred another.

"We're gonna have to call the police," I said quietly. "It's no longer just pieces of paper."

I thought of the box at the very top of our closet, buried behind some old blankets, and what was secreted away inside.

Trent made a sound and downshifted. "I need to see them first."

I nodded, biting back the worry that maybe if we'd called them sooner, this wouldn't have happened.

4

Trent

The outside lights illuminated the massive main house, my eyes sweeping over the empty front porch as I braked to a stop right beside the SUV Travis had been driving and killed the engine. Yanking the keys and unclipping my seat belt at the same time, I moved to get out.

"Trent." Drew's hand on my arm stopped me.

I said nothing, just looked over my shoulder.

"Put your dick away, frat boy."

It took a second, and then I glanced down, seeing my open jeans and soft cock half out of the waistband of my boxers.

"Shit," I exclaimed, sitting back so I could quickly stuff it back in my pants.

"We might be in a hurry, but I don't share."

I let out a sound, a cross between a laugh and a groan, and lunged toward him, cupping his scruffy face between my palms. "I'm sorry our date got cut short, baby. I still want to talk. I want to hear every word in that beautiful brain of yours."

He nodded, the action moving my arms with his head. "I know."

"You'll always be my favorite," I whispered as if it wasn't the world's worst-kept secret.

His dimple appeared, charming in every circumstance. "I know."

"Let's go inside," I prompted.

I expected Drew to fall into step with me the second I was around the hood, but he wasn't there, and I peered around to see him inspecting the SUV.

"What is it?" I asked, nerves and anger so tight in my stomach it made me feel nauseous. "Is there damage?" My hands shook with the thought of my kids in a car chase with someone vengeful and desperate enough to approach a little girl eating ice cream to spew lies.

"No, everything looks good," Drew announced. "Just making sure."

The front door swung open, and Andi rushed out. "Daddy!"

I took off, feet rushing over pavement to get to my daughter. Even out here in the dark, I could see the tear tracks on her cheeks.

When I was close enough, she launched herself at me, leaping as though the steps weren't even there or as if she had complete trust in me that I'd catch her regardless.

It only fed the dark part of me that would do anything to keep her safe.

The breath whooshed out of me, and I stumbled back when I plucked her out of the air. She was just a little peanut, but she weighed a lot more than she used to. Drew was there with a steadying hand on my back and posture braced to keep us both up if needed.

The second my arms went around our daughter, she let out a cry and buried her face in my neck. The length of her dark hair tangled in my fingers and brushed over my forearm when I palmed the back of her head.

Sobs racked her little frame, and her arms trembled with the force with which she clung to me.

I closed my eyes and breathed deep, trying desperately to stomp down the rage coiling in every part of my body.

"You're okay," I murmured, rubbing her back. "I got you."

"Daddy," she wailed, crying all over again. Her tears smeared against my neck, hurt seeping into my skin.

Holding her tight, I pivoted to Drew, searching for that blue gaze to ground me.

He was my other half. I didn't have to say a word. He knew. He felt the same. We were two halves of the same soul.

His chest brushed my arm and side, one hand going to the back of my hand and the other to Andi. "Hey, baby girl, we're here now."

Sniffling, she swiped her wet face across my shoulder and reached for Drew, melting into his arms to bury her face in his neck the same way she'd done mine.

I watched them for a second, my heart swelling to near painful. He whispered something in her ear, and she nodded, and he kissed her on the head. "How about we go inside? You can tell us what's up."

She nodded again and then twisted to reach for me. I glanced at Drew, and he smiled knowingly. I tucked her into my chest and carried her up the steps and through the front door.

Inside, the air was warm and scented with vanilla. The hum of a TV played in the background, and the sound of the running dishwasher filtered in from the kitchen.

Two dogs came rushing up, one of them Ketchup, both of them smelling Andi's foot as if to make sure she was okay.

Romeo was sitting on the steps leading upstairs, and we locked eyes immediately.

"Lo?"

"She's okay."

I nodded. "I'm sorr—"

He cut me off before I could finish, standing. "Don't." He shook his blond head.

Since retiring from pro football, he'd grown it out a little and slacked off on the shaving. Both he and Drew were blond-haired, blue-eyed, and now scruffy, but only one of them affected me.

"You didn't do anything to be sorry for."

The door shut behind me, and Drew came forward. "Where's Travis?"

Romeo hitched a chin toward the living room, and we turned.

He was across the room by the window, standing between the parted curtains to stare out at the driveway and trees. From his position, I knew he saw us pull up and Andi leaping into my arms.

The back of his dark head was motionless, his shoulders tense and arms folded in front of him. He was dressed in his usual style of black everything.

Drew was right. He was a strong kid. There was nothing wrong with strength. Strength was a good thing.

Except people tended to forget that strength was usually a product of pain. That strength was sometimes your only choice.

The world breaks all of us in one way or another, and it broke my son far earlier than most. Those broken spots healed into thick scars, like iron thrown into the fire to be forged into something stronger.

I never wanted my son's strength to overshadow his pain, for him to think it was one or the other because, often in life, it never was.

I turned to my husband, our daughter between us. He held out his arms. "Come here, peanut."

Andi went willingly, and Drew motioned to Trav with his head.

Chest tight, I put my back to the room, to everyone but my son. "Travis."

His shoulders moved a few inches toward his ears, but otherwise, he remained still. I felt the emotion rolling off him in waves, could practically taste the hurricane within him. But Trav was an enigma, and I wasn't sure what kind of storm this was or what exactly he was feeling. I might understand he was broken, but our breaks were not the same.

"There's no one out at the gate," I told him. "No one inside it either. Didn't see anyone on my way in."

Nothing.

"Any trouble getting home?"

He shook his head once.

"You hurt?"

Another sharp shake of his head.

"You wanna turn around and look at me?"

Nothing.

"You know we aren't mad at you, right?"

The spike in the energy around him told me I was getting closer to the eye of his storm.

I shifted a little, enough that I could see his reflection in the glass. His jaw was locked, dark eyes staring straight ahead. Sometimes I wondered what those obsidian eyes saw because the opaque depths kept everything a secret.

"It was scary, huh?" I said, quieter than before. "Watching someone approach your sister. Trying to take her away."

His lower lip disappeared beneath his teeth.

"We aren't mad, Trav. We're proud of you."

He turned then, so swift the curtains swayed, and he

collided into me like I was a punching bag. He didn't wrap his arms around me, just full-body barreled into me, his face turned into my chest with his hands at his sides.

I wrapped around him immediately, thinking it would be better if this were Drew. Drew gave the best hugs on the planet. But then one of the hands at his sides lifted just enough to grab onto the hem of my T-shirt. I might not have noticed if not for the tension in the fabric at my shoulder.

Water pressed at the backs of my eyes, making my vision blur and my head feel tight. I stared ahead, thinking of the five-year-old who would hide behind my leg when life got to be too much.

I opened and closed my mouth, attempting to release some of the pressure in my head as I hunched in and hugged him harder. *I'm sorry I didn't get to you sooner.*

If I had one regret in life, it was that.

"I hit her," he said, the words muffled against my shirt.

I forced myself not to react even though everything inside me stilled. Cupping the back of his head, I leaned in. "Who?"

"The woman who tried to take Andi."

"You hit her?" I repeated, heart beating painfully hard.

His cheek rubbed against my chest when he nodded.

I held him tighter. Being a parent didn't come with a manual. It was hard to know what to do and what to say. Especially when you just wanted to protect them, when you loved them no matter what.

"I'm supposed to control my temper. I'm not supposed to fight. And she was a girl."

"What was she doing when you hit her?" I asked, holding back the urge to tell him it was okay. I mean, it *was* okay. That fucking hag hurt my daughter. But in order to give him the acceptance he truly needed, I had to listen first.

"I told her to back off. To get away from us. She wouldn't

listen and was causing a scene. She grabbed Andi's arm, made her spill her ice cream."

My stomach twisted. Against his back, my hands balled into fists.

"She dragged her out of her chair and onto the sidewalk. No one touches my sister," he said, lifting his head until those bottomless black eyes gazed right into mine, his short dark lashes nothing but a punctuation to that penetrating stare. "No one hurts my sister."

"I know." I agreed. "And then what?"

"I tackled her. Sacked her just like I would a player on the field. She went down hard, and when I got up, she grabbed my hand. I smacked her off me. Then I got Andi and London and got out of there."

His eyes slid over to the side. "I didn't speed. Even if I did want to."

Drew's shoulder lightly brushed mine when he stepped forward. "I trust you."

"We're proud of you," I repeated. "You did exactly the right thing. Violence is never the answer, but sometimes it's necessary. You had to protect yourself and the girls."

He glanced up, and it was like staring down at that five-year-old from so long ago. "Really?"

"Yeah, really, bud," I said, dragging him into another hug. It didn't even matter that he didn't use his arms because he sank into me with his whole body. I dipped my face. "I'm proud of you, son. I'll always be on your side."

His body moved with the force of his relief as though the worst of the storm was over and now he could breathe.

I looked at Drew, my anchor in every storm. A beat passed between us.

He came forward, wrapped his arms around us both, and squeezed. *Ah, that's the stuff.*

"So is no one going to acknowledge the kid used the

moves I taught him on the football field to bring that woman down?" Braeden disrupted the quiet.

I looked over my shoulder.

The entire family was sitting there in the living room.

There was no privacy in this place.

"*Who* taught my son how to play football?" I inquired. *Me, that's who.*

B made a face. "Uh, his coach." He pointed to himself. "And for the record, Trav, I don't think she counts as a girl. She might identify as a woman, but from where I'm sitting, she's a criminal. Her pronouns are delinquent/dangerous/asking for it."

"You aren't even sitting," Ivy muttered.

Drew snickered.

"Baby, if you wanted me to sit down, you could have said so," he told her, going over to the couch to pick her up and sit down with her in his lap.

"Uh, Dads?" Travis called.

I glanced down at the teenager still squished between us.

"Oops," Drew said, and we both stepped back to give him some air.

"Don't do that again," Travis told us, cheeks red with embarrassment. "I'm getting a soda."

He fled from the room like his Nikes were on fire, and Drew and I turned toward the fam. Andi was sitting under a blanket with Rimmel, and London was on Romeo's lap.

"You know what to do," I told him.

He smiled. "Family meeting!"

5

Drew

"Uncle Braeden, what's pronouns?" Andi asked as we all settled in for another one of Rome's family meetings.

They were just as frequent as pancake Sundays around here.

B made a choked sound.

Romeo laughed out loud. "You walked right into that one, man."

"Yeah, Uncle Braeden, do tell," Rimmel said, pushing the glasses up on her nose.

Ivy twisted to stare at Braeden, expecting an explanation.

"Words we use to describe a person without using their name," Braeden told her. "Yours are princess/peanut/precious."

"What are mine?" London asked like it was some kind of game.

"Oh, that's easy," B said. "Angel/strawberry/smalls junior."

"He's just making stuff up," Nova told the girls. "It's the terms we use for a person's gender identity. Mine are she/her like both of you. Jax's are he/him just like all the other boys. Some people don't identify as a girl or a boy, so theirs would be they/them."

"Mine are funner," B said, and Ivy elbowed him.

"This conversation is entertaining and all, but can we get back to the stuff we need to discuss?" T said. He was clearly still in protective alpha mode, and frankly, it was sexy.

He was totally one of those DILFs.

DILF = Dad I'd Like to Fuck.

Romeo sat forward, Lolo still tucked into his lap. She seemed even smaller against his large frame, and my stomach tightened thinking of her and Andi in the crosshairs of some money-hungry psycho.

Unable to shake the unsettling image, I went to where Andi and Rimmel were tucked under a blanket and lifted the corner. "You got any room under there?"

Andi pulled the blanket back and stood up, her sock-covered feet sinking into the oversized couch cushions. I sat down, and she plopped into my lap. Rimmel tucked the blanket around us and leaned her head on my shoulder.

I'd never survive if something happened to them.

Whipped by fear, I sought out Trent to find he was already looking at me. Our eyes connected, and I knew he knew what I was thinking.

His eyes slipped to our daughter and then back to the room. "We need to take care of this. Efficiently."

"What's going on?" Blue asked, picking up the heavy vibes in the room.

Some of the kids hadn't been in the room until Romeo called the meeting.

"Travis took the girls out for ice cream earlier tonight,"

Romeo replied. "And while they were there, a woman approached Andi."

"She didn't approach her. She came up to the table and yanked her away, tried to put her in her car," Travis said, clearly still rattled.

A sense of helplessness enveloped me. *I should have been there.*

Nova gasped. "Someone tried to kidnap Andi?"

"She said she was my mom," Andi said, looking up at me. "And that you and Daddy took me from her."

Trent started to pace, a dark scowl twisting his face.

"She's not our mom, Andi," Travis deadpanned. "Our mom is dead."

"Travis," Trent snapped.

"It's true."

"Doesn't mean you need to say it like that."

"I know she's dead, Trav," Andi shot back. Turning confused, upset eyes on me, she asked, "But why would she say that?"

We've never made a secret of them being adopted. It was openly talked about and part of them, part of our story as a family. It made no sense to tiptoe around it and try to sugar-coat where they came from—especially since Travis was five when we found him. Even though Andi had been just a baby and wouldn't remember, Trav did. Asking him not to talk about any of it around her would be like telling him he had to be ashamed of where they came from.

These kids had nothing to be ashamed of. They were survivors. Fighters. I was proud as hell of them, and I would never say otherwise.

Yes, their story was hurtful and dark, but learning to own and accept it was part of life. Knowing we loved and accepted them no matter what was something we worked hard to teach them.

However.

Trying to explain to an eleven-year-old why some batshit insane woman tried to kidnap her was not easy.

"Remember how we told you that some people might try and take advantage of us?" I asked.

"Because you're famous and rich?"

"Yeah, because I drive race cars and am on TV sometimes. And your uncles were famous football players. Aunt Ivy is in magazines."

"And Mom saves animals," Lolo put in.

"That's right, strawberry. Because your mom is an angel," Romeo answered.

"Uncle B said I'm an angel," Andi said.

Seriously, my girl was so angelic I could practically see her halo. My throat was too tight to swallow, so I nodded and glanced at Rim whose eyes shimmered behind her glasses. Clearing my throat, I said, "You must get that from her."

Trent appeared, dragging back the coffee table so he could drop onto his knees in front of the couch. One of his hands fell on my knee, and the other reached for our daughter. "Some people are jealous, and they want to have the stuff we have. It makes them do things they shouldn't. Bad things."

"Like lie?" she asked.

Trent nodded. "That wasn't your mom, baby. Your mom passed away not long after you were born."

She nodded, familiar with the truth. "And Trav took care of me until you and Daddy came."

Listen, we didn't talk about the part where her mom was a raging drug addict and Andi was born with neonatal abstinence syndrome. Just because it wasn't a secret didn't mean we needed to divulge every detail. She was still a child.

Trav knew, though. Trav watched his mom overdose.

Trent nodded. "Yeah. And we have all the official paperwork that says you're our daughter. We didn't take you from anyone."

Andi nodded. "I belong here with you and Daddy."

He nodded. "You can see the papers again," Trent offered. "Anytime you want."

"I don't need to see the papers, Daddy. Papers don't make us family." She laid her hand over her chest. "Our hearts do."

Someone sniffled somewhere in the room. I didn't bother looking. I couldn't. My entire being was riveted on my husband's face when my daughter repeated the words he always said back to him.

And though he didn't move an inch, he crumbled.

A storm of emotion rewrote his expression. His eyes were stripped bare and openly raw. The guard he was always armored with fell, giving an unprecedented look at the softness shielded behind his heart. A place I'd only seen myself a handful of times, a place so delicate it was basically an open wound that would never heal.

His lower lip trembled just slightly, and then he cleared his throat. "Come here," he rasped, reaching for her.

She went right to him, folding her arms around his neck and wrapping her legs around his torso when he stood. She looked like a little koala clinging to a massive tree.

I rubbed my chest, the ache there so intense I could barely breathe.

The room was thick. Everyone was still, the intensity of T's emotion overriding everything else.

He walked toward the fireplace, big hand rubbing up and down her back. "I love you so goddamn much," he said, voice thick. "Don't ever doubt that."

"I don't need a mom anyway. You and Daddy are better."

His footsteps halted, and he swayed on his feet. He

dropped his face to her tiny shoulder, and I watched his shoulders rise and fall.

Untangling from the blanket, I stood and went to them. The second my hand slid across his back, his muscles tensed. "Why don't we make some coffee?" I suggested quietly.

He nodded.

"Can I have some?" Andi asked.

"Yes," Trent replied instantly. She could ask him for a pony right now and he'd go out and get three.

"I think it's a little late for you to have coffee, peanut. It will keep you awake half the night," I said, tugging her from his arms.

"Won't it keep you awake?" she asked.

"No, I'm old." I lied.

She didn't need to know I wouldn't be sleeping tonight anyway.

I turned, and Romeo was right there, blue eyes knowing.

"Here, go sit with Uncle Romeo while we get some coffee."

"Can I have a cookie?" she asked. "My ice cream fell on the ground."

T made a noise behind us, and I handed her over to Rome. "I'll bring you a cookie."

Romeo tickled her as soon as she was in his arms, and she laughed, the sound too innocent for this world. The second he sat down, Ketchup leaped up on the couch and laid his head in her lap.

"Come on, frat boy," I murmured, tugging him toward the kitchen.

"Let's go over safety protocol," Braeden told the room.

A few kids groaned.

"We know, Dad!" Jax moaned. "You've told us a thousand times."

"It's time for a reminder," Romeo said. "Now listen up."

"Safety protocol didn't stop my daughter from almost being abducted," Trent muttered, voice dark.

I'd been expecting this. The break in his calm, cool exterior. I just expected it later tonight when we were alone.

"I know," I murmured, settling a hand between his shoulder blades. "But it's still shit they need to know."

"If Travis hadn't been there," Trent whispered and looked up with wild eyes.

"I know, baby," I murmured, pulling him in to wrap my arms around him. "They're okay, though. They're all okay."

"Did you hear what she said?" His voice broke.

"Pretty sure it tattooed itself on my heart."

"Mine too." He agreed, wrapping his arms around me. "How is it she's the one who almost got hurt and I'm the one falling apart?"

I smiled over his shoulder, staring toward the cabinets. Ivy had new ones installed last year. I still wondered what was wrong with the old ones.

"You aren't falling apart, T. You're just getting a glimpse at how well you love our kids."

He pulled back just enough to see me. "You love them too. We all do."

I half smiled. "Of course we do. But there's something about your love, T. It hits different."

He shook his head, and I grabbed his face to kiss him.

He relaxed against me, and I carded my hands through his hair while slipping him a little tongue. His edges seemed smoother when I pulled back, swiping my thumb along his lower lip.

"I'm making you some coffee," I told him and turned to grab a pod out of the basket on the counter next to the fancy Nespresso machine.

If you asked me, these were just a marketing gimmick. And probably bad for the environment. Sure, these little pods were recyclable, but how many people do you think actually recycled them? Not many. Wankers.

Besides, coffee in an old-fashioned pot tasted better. If it ain't broke, don't fix it. You could pry my Mr. Coffee out of my cold, dead hands. Though, you'd get it easier than my fries.

That being said, this stupid machine was nice for brewing a single cup. It was kinda late in the day for a whole pot.

After slipping the pod into the machine and hitting the button, I watched it begin to brew. Trent wrapped around me from behind, his body pressing me against the counter.

"I want you," he rumbled beside my ear.

All the hair on my body stood on end. Jolts of desire shot through me like my nervous system was experiencing an electrical storm. Leaning into him, I reached around and slid my hand into the back pocket of his jeans.

"You have me."

When he shifted, his hard dick stabbed against my ass. "What else am I supposed to do with all this pent-up emotion, baby? I need somewhere to put it."

I arched against him. "Lucky for you, I have just the place."

"I am lucky."

I turned in his arms. "No, T. You deserve everything you have."

He leaned in to kiss me, and I slipped away, grabbing his cup and going to the fridge for some creamer. When it was made the way he liked it, I handed it over.

"After we talk to the kids more, I think we need to involve the police."

"Yeah. I think you're right."

"They're going to want to talk to the kids. Get a description from them of this woman."

"Not tonight. Andi's been through enough."

I nodded. "I'll call down there and see if they can come out tomorrow. Doing it at home might be easier for them."

"T?"

"Hm?"

"Do you think we did the wrong thing by not contacting them about the letters?" I asked, the mere suggestion a knife to my gut.

His attention went inward as he considered my words. I waited on pins and needles for what he would say. It wasn't that I didn't have my own thoughts, just that I valued his a little more. As I said before, he was our rock.

After a sip of the coffee, he shook his head. "No. I think drawing attention to it would have caused more panic. And if it got out to the press, it would have become a circus."

"And inspired copycats."

"Exactly." He agreed.

"I still feel guilty," I confessed.

Trent cupped the side of my face, scratching against my beard. "Because you're a good father. But you didn't do anything wrong."

The compliment made me warm inside, and I pulled the coffee from his hand to help myself. He let me have it and went to the cupboard to rummage around. When he came back, it was with an entire pouch of cookies.

"She only asked for one."

"And?"

I laughed. "You are wrapped around her tiny finger." Shaking my head, I started back to the meeting, still drinking his coffee.

Coffee sloshed over the rim and splashed my hand when I was yanked back. I barely noticed the warm liquid stinging my skin because of the distracting body pressed against me and the hot whisper against my ear.

"Later, I want you wrapped around my dick."

Desire slid down my spine, making me shiver.

"Dad! Where's my cookie?" Andi hollered.

"Later," he promised and pulled away to see to our daughter. Before I could join them, I had to reach into my jeans to adjust the rigid dick behind my fly.

6

Trent

Three months ago, we started getting letters.

Typed words on plain white paper in a standard envelope and mailed to our house.

There was a woman out there claiming to be Travis and Andi's mother. At first, she tried the *woe-is-me* approach, claiming her kids were taken unfairly because she got into trouble and, when she was out, they were lost in the system.

According to her, she searched for them for years and only found them when she saw a photo of Andi in some tabloid—an *unauthorized* photo, I might add. I will also add that this was exactly why you don't take pictures of kids. Fucking vultures.

We ignored the first letter. And the second.

The third was more desperate in tone, begging us to let her see her children and claiming it wasn't fair that we were keeping her away.

We ignored that one too, hoping she'd get bored and stop.

The fourth letter demanded money. She wanted half a million, or she was going to the press to tell everyone we took her kids.

That one was harder to ignore, but we did. The cops would say it was a baseless threat, a weak attempt to extort money from a celebrity. Since there was no physical threat and no basis at all for her claims, we didn't want to give her the attention she sought by going to the press or police.

Plus, we didn't want to scare our kids.

It wasn't the first time we'd been stalked by paps trying to get photos or overzealous fans wanting Drew's autograph. Hell, one time someone waited at the track for us to come out after a race and insisted he was Drew's long-lost twin brother and they'd been separated at birth.

An introduction to my fist seemed to knock the sense back into that bozo. Or maybe he just knew I'd do worse than punch him if he came around again.

The fourth letter was weeks ago. When a fifth didn't come, I hoped the woman had given up.

She gave up, all right. Gave up sending letters and graduated to direct contact with my child.

The next letter she sent? That would be from behind bars.

Kids had a right to be kids. Playing sports, going for ice cream, and hanging out with their friends was normal and probably something most parents didn't think twice about.

But for our kids, it came with safety protocol, limited social media access, and as of tonight, warnings about attempted kidnapping.

After the meeting, we left all seven of them on the sectional to watch a movie while the adults went into the kitchen for a more adult-style family meeting.

Ivy went directly to the freezer and pulled out a pint of Ben & Jerry's. Rimmel got out two spoons, and the pair started eating it at the island, right out of the container.

Braeden stared between them and then opened his mouth.

Ivy held up her spoon. "Not one word."

Rimmel tried to scoop out a bite, and a hunk of chocolate went flying across the counter and hit him in the chest.

Romeo grabbed it from where it landed and tossed it in his mouth. "Thanks, baby."

Rimmel giggled.

"Eating out of the carton. Making a mess." B shook his head. "When I do it, I get yelled at."

"You aren't as cute as they are," Romeo told him.

Braeden sighed dramatically. "Pretty privilege," he muttered, helping himself to a beer from the fridge. "Who else wants one?"

Romeo and Drew nodded, and when they each had one, B turned to me. "Trent?"

"No," I said. "I need to make a phone call." After grabbing my cell, I headed toward the sliders that led onto the back deck.

Before going out, I turned to Romeo. "You gonna be cool if the cops want to talk to Lolo about what happened tonight?"

The muscle in his jaw ticked, but he agreed.

I looked at my sister. "Rim?"

She laid her spoon down with a soft clink. "Of course. As long as we can be with her."

"We're all going to be there," Romeo said, voice steely. "I'll call my dad and have him come out in the morning. Wouldn't hurt to have our lawyer present."

I nodded.

"I'm calling security and adding extra to the gate and property perimeter," Braeden said.

"What should I do?" Drew asked.

"Stand there and look pretty," I said with a wink.

It was especially important to flirt with your person even when life was a shit circus. I learned that from Romeo.

Braeden snorted. "Pretty privilege."

"*Frat boy*," Drew intoned.

"Want some ice cream, Drew?" Ivy offered.

He scoffed. "I'm calling Gamble and getting the name of his private investigator. I'm not leaving it up to the cops to find this woman. I want her off the streets yesterday."

"You think he's awake at this time of night?" Rimmel worried.

"That man has more energy in his seventies than most men in their fifties," Drew purported. "It is late, though," he amended. "I'll call Lorhaven instead."

Drew followed me out onto the deck, and we made our calls on opposite ends. I was put through immediately to the chief and arranged for him and two of his deputies to come out to the compound in the morning.

Once finished, we met in the halo of illumination stretching across the deck boards through the window. Light and shadow cast across his face. The tip of his nose was pink from the cool air. Trees rustled in the distance, and the wind flirted with the blond tips of his hand-mussed hair.

Overhead, an abundance of stars made twinkling pinholes in the black velvet sky, but I only afforded them a passing glance because the man standing before me would always shine brighter.

The foot between us seemed too far, so I reached for his hand. "You talk to Lorhaven?"

He nodded. "I got the information. Offered to go out looking when they got here in a few days for Trav's party."

"She'll be in jail by then."

"You talk to the police?" Drew asked.

"Be here tomorrow at ten."

"I'm ready to go home, T."

Leaning into his space, I brushed a quiet kiss across his forehead. "Me too."

Our fingers stayed linked as we walked back inside to inform the fam of the news.

"Extra security is on the way," Braeden said.

"My dad will be here in the morning," Romeo added.

"Listen, Rome." I started, taking a step forward. "I'm sorry about this. That Lo was involved."

Rimmel made a stricken sound and leaped off the barstool. She would have face-planted if Romeo hadn't caught her around the waist, hauling her upright with one arm.

She didn't even pause, so accustomed to falling that it barely even fazed her. Her body collided with mine, arms winding around my waist and face buried in the middle of my chest.

Since Drew refused to give up custody of my hand, I wrapped my free arm around her.

"You don't have to apologize. No one expected this would happen." She spoke fiercely into my shirt.

"Well, it did, and that's your daughter," I replied, still meeting Romeo's gaze.

"Your daughter was there too," he answered. "And your son."

"I'm proud of that kid," Braeden said. "He protected our girls."

"He shouldn't have had to." My voice was harsh. Christ, he was sixteen years old. That was too much responsibility to put on a kid.

Drew's fingers tightened around mine, and Rimmel lifted her head, brown eyes wide.

"Sorry for yelling, sis," I murmured and patted her on the head. My wedding band got caught in the strands.

"Ow!" she said, reaching up.

I tried to pull my hand free again, but she grabbed my wrist.

"We're stuck," she declared. "Romeo! I'm stuck."

Romeo shook his head. "You're killing me, smalls."

"You should really think about combing your hair," I told her.

She snorted. "Like that helps. It just goes back to this anyway."

I laughed, and it eased the worst of the pressure in my chest. When she smiled, I found myself smiling back.

"I got this," Drew announced, finally relinquishing my hand so he could use both of his to untangle us. "I love ya, sis, but I draw the line at sharing my man."

"This is ridiculous," Rimmel muttered, trying to tug free. "*Ow.*"

Drew tsked. "Gonna need the butter."

Ivy gasped. "You will *not* put butter in her hair!"

"Basically the same thing as conditioner," Drew reasoned.

"You know it's true," Braeden wisecracked.

Ivy gasped again. "I am embarrassed to be married to you."

"That hurts my feelings, blondie."

"Good."

She squealed when Braeden snatched her off the stool and tossed her over his shoulder. "We're going to bed. Someone needs a reminder of why I'm the best husband on the planet."

"He wishes," Drew muttered. Suddenly, my hand pulled free from Rim's knotted hair. "You're free," he announced.

"Braeden James, put me down," Ivy exclaimed, slapping him on the back.

"Just a little lower next time, sweetheart."

"Meeting tomorrow at ten." I reminded them.

"We'll be here," B called.

"Good night!" Rimmel yelled as she smoothed out her hair.

"Ew, Dad!" Jax exclaimed a moment later, clearly getting an eyeful of his parents' shenanigans. "That's just gross."

"We're going to bed," Braeden told them.

"TMI, Dad!" Nova hollered. "TMI!"

"Breakfast at nine!" Ivy called as Braeden's footfalls hit the stairs. "Don't stay up too late."

"Come over here before you get caught on something else," Romeo murmured, pulling Rim into his arms and wrapping them around her.

"We're going home," I told them. "We'll see you in the morning."

"Trent." Romeo's voice made me stop and turn. "We're gonna deal with this like we do everything else. As a family."

I nodded, and we went into the family room where I found Andi asleep against Travis's shoulder while he hammered an Xbox controller with his fingers. My heart felt like a giant bruise seeing them like that.

"Time to go," I whispered, reaching down to lift Andi. She stirred long enough to wind her thin arms around my neck before falling back into dreamland.

Trav handed the controller off to Blue and stood, following us out the front door.

In the driveway, Drew tossed him the keys to the fastback. "Can you drive this down to the house? I'm gonna ride with your dad and sister."

Travis's eyes rounded. "For real?"

It was the first time Drew had ever let him drive his baby without supervision.

"Unless you don't want to—" Drew began.

"No." Trav was quick to deny. "I do."

"See you at home," Drew called and then went around to open the passenger side of the SUV.

"It doesn't make up for what he went through tonight," Drew said as I slid into the seat and adjusted Andi who still snored.

"No, but he's thrilled as shit," I mused.

Drew's gaze slid over our daughter, a flicker of worry flashing in his eyes. Shifting closer, he smoothed some of her hair and tugged the hem of her shirt to make sure it covered her completely. "She should be wearing a jacket."

"It's a short drive home."

The sound of the fastback roaring to life made Drew look up, a smile tugging at his lips.

We followed Travis the short distance to our house, which had gone through a few changes over the years just like the main house. The biggest having been the addition we put on after our first Christmas as a family of four.

What was supposed to be a simple addition of a couple bedrooms and a bathroom turned into a full-on renovation when Ivy got wind of the project. Apparently, we needed a game room, a library for studying, and Andi needed a walk-in closet and her own bathroom. It was a girl thing, ya know.

Except I didn't know because Trav got his own bathroom too.

So really, it was an all-gender thing.

I didn't ask. I just did as Ivy said.

The family room and kitchen got upgrades, so there was more room to make reindeer food (and you know, actual food), space for a gigantic Christmas tree, and a massive mantel for hanging stockings. We even added a deck of our own off the back and a smaller version of the firepit up at the main house.

Then a few years ago, we added onto the garage in anticipation of the kids getting cars someday… which was basically today because soon, Trav would have his own Mustang parked inside.

Yeah, yeah, the insurance on a car like that for a seventeen-year-old boy was going to be astronomical.

I didn't give a damn.

If I could slow down time, I would. But then I'd have to trade in all the memories we'd made over the last decade, so instead, I'd just look forward to the memories yet to come.

After tucking Andi into bed and making sure she was sleeping peacefully, I said good night to Trav and went into our bedroom where Ketchup was sprawled across the center of the bed and snoring like a lawnmower.

He barely even twitched when I walked by, and I just shook my head on the way to the bathroom and the running shower. I slid through the narrow opening, gently closing it behind me as warm, steamy air greeted my skin. The strong scent of soap promised to wash away the worst of the day as I stripped my shirt and shucked my pants, tossing them near the vanity where Drew's already lay.

The mirror was fogged up and so was the glass shower door, the cascade of water a rhythmic cadence that resonated through the enclosed space. The sound, scent, and dewy air combined, creating a white-noise effect that muffled any competing sounds without being so loud that it was intrusive.

The muscles in my back began unclenching as I reached for the handle to glide open the door.

Drew didn't turn but acknowledged my presence with a low hum and passed the soap over his shoulder. Moving up behind him, I took the offering and rubbed the sudsy bar between my palms before laying them against his back.

His wet head dropped toward his chest, and I worked him over, massaging the soap over his tense skin until it was pliant. Clouds of steam created a veil, and water splashed against my feet and calves as I worked my way down to his hips and well-defined ass.

"Didn't we just do this, this morning?" I murmured, fingers sliding through his crack.

"It feels like so long ago," Drew whispered, widening his stance so I'd have more room.

The tile was unforgiving and wet when I lowered to my knees. Starting with his ankles, I worked up each leg, kneading the muscles and soaping his skin until suds dripped between us to swirl in the water puddled on the floor.

He moaned quietly, leaning his arms against the wall and resting his head on them, giving up his body to my hands. The offering of his lower half was too tempting to deny, and I abandoned the soap to fill my hands with his cheeks and pull them apart.

Rivulets of water ran across his lower back and through his newly bared crack, making him drip and glisten.

His moan echoed through the room when I licked up the center then dove in without hesitation. Drew was *really* into oral stimulation. Dude had always been a sucker for a blow job, but as the years went on, I realized he loved my mouth on him anywhere he could get it. He also really loved having his mouth on me.

I circled my tongue around his rim, slurping up the water gathering there and prodding his entrance with the tip. Hissing, he pushed back hard enough that I penetrated slightly. A shiver rolled through his body, and I dug my fingers into his hips and tugged.

"Shit," he rasped when my tongue went deeper, and I swirled and thrust into his opening.

I loved the little sounds he made. Like he was helpless against the way I made him feel. I kept at him, teasing his hole and then sucking on the rim until it was loose and his knees were quivering. Turning my face, I kissed across his cheek and around to his hip, nibbling on the skin while dipping a finger into his body.

"Please, T," he whispered, reaching around to dig his fingers into my arm.

"Please, what?"

A frustrated sound bounced off the tiles. "You know."

Withdrawing, I stood slowly, and Drew straightened slightly to deliver a disgruntled glare over his shoulder.

"*T*," he whined, and I snatched him from behind and yanked, bringing his wet, naked body right against mine.

I held him tight around the waist with one arm and wrapped my free hand around the front of his throat, applying just enough pressure to feel an uptake in his breathing.

I held him tight enough that I knew my dick was stabbing him and he could feel every part of me from shoulder to thigh. Leaning in, I sucked his ear between my lips, and he squirmed in my hold.

"I know what you need, baby. I'm right here to give it to you."

His chest rose and fell heavily as I slid the hand at his waist lower to grab his cock. Water poured over us as I slid up and down, turning my wrist just a little at the tip.

His hand went behind us, fingers digging into my ass, trying to pull me closer. His dick was hot beneath the water, so hard it seemed to have a pulse of its own.

I thrust against him, sliding my dick along his crack, fucking into him without breaching his hole.

Another impatient sound rumbled in his throat, but before it could make it out, I pushed two fingers into his mouth right against his tongue. He locked onto them, sucking as if his life depended on it, and I used the distraction to grab the lube behind the shampoo and pour it all over my cock. The second the cool, slippery liquid hit his crack, he pulled off my fingers and bent, practically showing me his ass.

Gripping the sides of his narrow waist, I pushed through the tight ring with one solid thrust. Both of us groaned, and my abs flexed so tight that a wave of nausea rolled over me. But then it was gone, and I buried myself until our skin met and I was completely inside him.

He purred, and I pushed his shoulders down, letting water rain over his back and sluice off his hips. My eyes lingered on the lines of his body, how he made a perfect V, and then lower to where my body invaded his.

Slowly, I pulled back, eyes fixated and completely obsessed with the way his ass tried to suck me back in. After that, I unleashed, letting loose the part of me that needed to claim him. I pounded into him, our grunts and slapping skin making a rhythm of their own.

Even though we were in the shower, beads of sweat formed on my hairline and lower back. The muscles in my thighs strained, but I didn't stop chasing the high that was Drew's body.

When he started to slide down the wall, I yanked him back against me. His back to my chest, his head fell back so I could feel his panting breaths as we strained together.

"Come for me, baby," I rasped, straining onto tiptoes as I fought the urge to let go.

Drew felt around and then grabbed my hand, yanking it to his dick. "Hold me," he whispered.

I slid my hand up his shaft and cupped his head. "Give it to me, Drew. Fill me up."

His entire body bowed, and I ground against him, rubbing that magic spot I knew so well. He shuddered and shook while cum splashed my fingers and puddled in my hand.

And then I was coming too, white-hot pleasure searing me from the inside out as my orgasm roared out of my tip and into his channel.

When we both came back, we were slumped against the shower wall, my dick still buried inside him and my fist full of cum.

Exhaling thickly, I kissed over his shoulder and to the base of his neck. He tilted his head, and I took the opportunity to suck a bruise right above his collarbone.

When I lifted my head, Drew turned to cuddle into my chest. I hugged him close before pulling back so we could kiss long, slow, and deep while warm water rained over our tangled limbs.

"I love you," I whispered.

"I love you more," he whispered back.

I didn't even bother to tell him it just wasn't possible.

7

Drew

You know what I liked about my sister? Besides everything—though her choice in men was questionable—it was her keen eye for good stuff.

Yeah, yeah, you could argue that Braeden also qualified as "good stuff," but I wasn't arguing. I was too comfortable.

You know why I was too comfortable? Besides the fact that I was naked and in T's arms.

Wait. What the hell is wrong with me? Going on and on instead of getting to the point.

Dick-drunk.

Mmhmm, T put me out here in la-la land with that dick of his. Fuck, was he good at that.

Sheets. I'm trying to tell you that the sheets covering our California king bed were utter perfection. Soft, slightly silky, and cool to the touch. Slipping between them without a scrap of fabric covering my body was one of life's many pleasures. The blanket and duvet over them were also top-notch, so much so that Andi called our bed a fluffy cloud.

After a long day, being tucked between these high-quality threads with my naked man was pretty much perfection. I mean, I didn't even miss French fries.

What did this have to do with Ivy? She'd picked out all this bedding, duh. Girl was a certified shopaholic.

Trent's palm grazed along the side of my thigh, curving over my hip and settling where my waist dipped in above it. "What's going on in that blond head of yours?"

"I like this bed," I replied, voice sounding just as dick-drunk as the rest of me felt.

Right after our heated shower, we hastily dried and stumbled into bed in the dark. Overhead, the ceiling fan whirred, and Ketchup snored at the foot of the bed. We were on our sides facing each other, blankets piled high and creating a soft separation between us and the rest of the world.

"I like you in this bed."

There he went again. A professional one-upper. Probably why Gamble kept giving him raises.

"You think Andi will sleep through the night?" I asked. After what she'd gone through earlier, I'd be surprised if she did.

"We should probably put some clothes on just in case she crawls into bed with us."

"Not yet," I said, scooting closer until our chests were pressed together. "Five more minutes."

Trent laughed under his breath, the sexy rumble doing unexplained things to my insides. I draped my arm over his waist and pushed my leg between his. He tugged me closer, adjusting so his leg was pinning my lower half and his arm was around me with nimble fingers carding through my damp hair.

"People always talk about when babies won't sleep

through the night or when they hit the terrible twos," I murmured, drawing patterns on Trent's chest with my fingers. "No one ever talks about how hard it is when your kids get older. When they want to use that independence you tried so hard to teach them. You suddenly worry that you weren't enough and the world is just too cruel."

Trent's entire hand enveloped the back of my head, rubbing against my scalp as he hummed over my words. "There is not a timeline in the entire universe where you are not enough."

"I want to be home more," I confessed.

Trent pulled back just enough so he could search my face. "You mean retiring from racing?"

I nodded. "I've been thinking about it for a while. The kids are getting older. Travis is a senior this year. Andi is practically a teenager."

"She's eleven." Trent amended.

"Almost twelve," I refuted. "And tonight was scary as fuck. It just made me even more convinced that this is the right move."

"We're gonna find this woman," he said, absolute conviction in his voice. "I will not stop until she's punished for what she did tonight."

"I know." I agreed. That woman didn't stand a chance with this family. But it wasn't just that. "I want to spend more time with them. I want to be at all of Trav's games and under the hood of the Mach 1 we're buying him. I want to take Andi to ballet and pick her up from school."

"You do that stuff now, baby."

I shook my head. "It isn't enough." I made a sound, frustrated that I couldn't quite put into words the way I felt. "I don't want my dreams to get in the way of theirs."

Trent pulled back, the whites of his eyes flashing in the dim room. "That's what you think?"

"No. Yes. I—"

Trent reached between us to grasp my chin. "You aren't him." His voice was gentle, but his eyes were firm. "Do you understand me, Drew?"

I never thought being a parent would give me daddy issues… but here I was.

A rough sound burst out of me, releasing pent-up pressure. "I know that." My heart squeezed with a fissure of panic, and I grappled for T's steadiness. "What if I turn into him, though?"

Trent's eyes softened, his face the picture of understanding and empathy. "How could that ever happen?" he asked, trying to understand my fear instead of denying it.

I appreciated that. The way Trent considered things instead of immediately dismissing them.

"With *him*..." I began, not saying his name. I'd never call him dad again. He lost the right to that title when he forced Trent away from my hospital bed. "It was always about what he wanted. He was so busy always trying to make everything the way he thought it should be, he never looked around to see how it could be. It was his way or no way, and for so long, I wanted his approval." My eyes bounced between Trent's. "He never asked me what I wanted. He never spent time learning about me. It's like…"

"Like what, baby?" T encouraged. *Listening*. Trent was always listening. If not with his ears, then his heart.

"He only knew the version of me he created. He never bothered to get to know the person I was."

And that hurt. It really fucking hurt.

Trent's thumb stroked across my cheekbone, and he leaned in, laying his lips on mine to quiet my silent heartbreak. I sighed into him, and he took the pain, kissing it away. The gentle coaxing of his tongue was unhurried and thorough in its comfort. Sometimes I didn't even know this shit was inside me until something happened and I was suddenly staring into its face.

Our lips broke apart with a soft suctioning sound, and his caressed my forehead when I dipped my chin.

"Even after all these years, I still don't know how to be a parent," I confessed quietly. "But I damn sure know what kind I don't want to be."

"For the record, I think our kids are fucking lucky to have you. And so am I."

I was the lucky one. "I've had it all," I answered. "The career of my dreams, money, kids. You. And you know what it's taught me?"

"What's that?"

"I don't need it all. Just you. And my kids."

"Driving is part of you," Trent said. "Motor oil in your veins, remember?"

I smiled. "I will always love driving, and I won't stop. I'll just shift gears a little. Besides, now that I'm forty, it's getting harder to keep all the young drivers off my taillights. I'd rather go out on top than leave because I start sucking."

Trent grinned. "You sound like Braeden."

My brother could have returned to football after a long recovery from his knee injury, but he knew he wouldn't be the same. I couldn't blame the dude for not wanting to watch his Hulk status shrivel.

"I admit, with him and Romeo both retired now… the grass is looking hella green on the other side."

"So what do you want to do?" Trent asked like he was opening a book of endless possibilities and telling me to pick one.

"For now, a dad and husband are enough. In the future? Who knows."

"I just want you to be happy, Drew. So if you're ready to retire and that will make you happy, I'm all for it."

"You won't miss being married to a pro driver?"

His lips twisted. "I think I can live without the constant worry for your safety."

"You almost die one time," I muttered sardonically.

"Once was way more than enough," Trent deadpanned.

He was right. It had been hell. Yet he still supported me when I made a comeback and didn't slow down since. I knew it was stressful for him, but he never complained.

"There is one thing I will miss," he said, a little tongue-in-cheek.

Color me intrigued. I met his eyes. "Yeah? What's that?"

"Your racing suit."

Surprise and humor rippled through me. "What?"

"So fucking hot."

I threw back my head and laughed. Wrapping my arms around him, I snuggled closer. "Is that why you always jump me after races?" I said, kissing along his jaw. "I just thought it was the adrenaline."

His hands reached around for my ass, digging his fingers into muscle. "A man has to keep some secrets."

I made a mental note to bring the suit home.

"T?" I asked, pulling back after some mild making out. "You sure you're okay with me retiring?"

"As long as you're doing it because *you* want to and not because you feel like you have to."

"This is what I want," I confirmed. After talking it out with my guy, I was even more convinced than before that this was what I wanted. Besides, I'd always be a driver.

I might be coming to the end of one track, but there was a whole highway out there I'd yet to travel.

8

Trent

The vibration of the phone against the nightstand roused me from sleep just enough for the sound to be annoying but not enough to make me open my eyes.

When it abruptly stopped, I slipped right back under as though I hadn't been interrupted at all.

Until it happened again.

This time, the sound didn't stop, the continuous vibration enough to make my eyes open. It was morning. I could tell that much by the light in the room, but it wasn't as bright as it usually was when my alarm went off.

I willed myself to silence the noise, but doing so required moving, and I quite liked where I was.

Gazing down, I took in the little peanut wrapped around my side, one leg thrown over mine. A brown bear was on my stomach, her arm tossed over both. Drew squished against my other side, his head pillowed on my shoulder, bedhead tickling my face. His arm was wrapped around Andi, the bear, and me.

Basically, I was the filling in a family sandwich.

Buzzzz, buzzzzz, buzzzzzz.

Drew groaned and brought his hand up to his face, trying to cover his ear. Dude was the worst morning person ever.

Sliding from under him, I snagged the phone and moved to silence the alarm. Except… my alarm wasn't going off. It wasn't supposed to go off for another forty minutes.

The buzzing was from a missed text, a couple Google alerts, and a missed call.

What the hell is going on?

Yawning, I swiped the sleep out of my eyes so I could read the screen. Before I could even pull up the notifications, the screen lit up in my hand.

Gamble's name flashed, and I sat up. Andi made a sound, so I quickly accepted the call to silence the ring.

Before answering, I got out of bed, nearly tripping over Ketchup's dog bed and a random shoe.

Cursing, I made sure Andi was covered and then headed for the hall.

"Ron?" I whispered the second I cleared the door. I'd been working with Gamble so long at the NRR that somewhere along the way, I stopped referring to him by his last name. "Is everything okay?"

"You're asking me?" he said, sounding more awake than Drew would ever be.

"Uh, yeah? You're the one calling before eight a.m.," I said, going downstairs. Goose bumps prickled my skin upon meeting the cold morning air, and I stopped to gaze out a window like I expected to see snow or something.

There was no snow, but the sky was overcast and gray. The leaves on the trees looked more golden than the day before, and a thick covering of fog made everything outside appear to be floating.

On my way to the kitchen, I flipped on the fireplace to help chase the early morning chill from the house and snagged a zip-up hoodie off the back of the sofa.

"What the hell is this, Mask?" Gamble demanded, which, by the way, was not an explanation.

"I'm afraid I don't follow," I replied, pushing one arm into the dark-colored sleeve.

"Well, that makes two of us then because I would have thought that if Drew was going to retire, he'd have the decency to call me before he made an announcement!"

My bare feet made a high-pitched squeaking sound when I halted. "*What*?"

"Look at your phone, Sleeping Beauty."

I pulled down the device and swiped to read my notifications. The first one that caught my eye was an alert for an article that went live less than an hour ago.

The end of the road for an icon?

Confused, I swiped to another.

Drew Mask retirement shocker!

"What the fuck?" I spat.

Is Drew Mask putting the brakes on his career?

Pushing the phone to my ear, I said, "Listen, Gamble, I have no idea how the press got wind of this. He literally just talked about it with me last night."

"So it's true?"

"We've talked about it." I hedged.

"You already said that."

"I think Drew should be the one to have this conversation with you."

"As if you two morons don't share a brain," Gamble muttered. "Is this because of what happened yesterday?" He went on.

"Yesterday?"

"Yet another thing no one called me about and I had to read in the papers."

I said nothing.

His sigh was exaggerated. "Look at the rest of your messages."

Daughter of NRR champion traumatized!

Attempted kidnapping foiled by sixteen-year-old boy—"He tackled her!"

Drew and Trent Mask's daughter in danger!

Drew forced from racing to protect his only daughter!

I let out a long line of expletives. "How the fuck did the press get ahold of this already?" I demanded.

"Witnesses from the ice cream shop," Gamble replied.

"They're printing photos, for chrissakes!" I roared, squeezing my phone so hard I was surprised the screen didn't crack. "She's a child!" I demanded. "A minor! So is Travis."

"I already have my lawyers on it." Gamble informed me.

"People have no fucking morals," I snapped, stomping over to the coffeemaker to brew a pot. "We haven't even spoken to the police."

His voice was sharp. "You didn't call them?"

"Of course we did. But we're meeting later this morning. The girls were too upset last night. So was Travis."

"Girls?"

"London was with them."

This time, Gamble cursed. "Why didn't you call?"

"It was late. Drew called Lorhaven for the PI's number. I called the cops, and Romeo and Braeden upped security."

"Good." He was gruff. "Still should have called me."

"I was going to call this morning."

"How are they?"

"Upset. The woman tried to drag Andi to her car. Travis got physical, stopping them."

"This about those bullshit letters?" he asked.

The entire family knew. Gamble, Lorhaven, Joey, Arrow, and Hopper, along with everyone up at the main house. Romeo's and B's parents knew too.

"Maybe we should have taken them more seriously," I whispered, looking over my shoulder to make sure no one was down here listening.

I didn't want anyone to think I doubted our decisions. Drew had enough going on in his head. I wasn't putting that on him. Besides, rationally, I knew we did the right thing. It was just hard because, well, we'd been wrong.

Gamble made a sound. "If we took every letter, call, or email we got seriously, we'd all be in early graves by now. I didn't make it this long in life by kowtowing to criminally insane demands. Hell, I'd be nothing but worm food by now after the first death threat I got in the nineties."

"I haven't even had coffee," I said, recoiling from that visual.

"You did what you thought was right. It's not your fault she's off her rocker."

"She had nightmares last night. Crawled into bed with us because she couldn't sleep," I confessed.

"I've already called my most reliable PI and a few others too," Gamble said. "They're already on her trail, and with the photos witnesses sold to the vultures, they have enough of a description to go on."

"I really appreciate it."

"That's what family does," Gamble deadpanned. "Anyone who traumatizes my grandkids will get my foot up their ass!" he declared. "And you tell Travis I'm proud of him! You know what? Never mind. I'll call him myself."

"He's still in bed."

"Young people these days. No respect for daylight. How do you think I got so rich? Sleep is for the lazy."

I made a noncommittal sound and poured some coffee. The rich scent permeating the room was a balm to my frazzled nerves.

How the hell did the press get wind of Drew considering retirement?

We'd only just talked about it ourselves. And in the comfort of our own bed.

Jesus, did someone have some kind of tap on our phones?

"Now what's this about Drew retiring?" Gamble cut into my thoughts. "I need to know if it's just fake news."

The diner.

I must have made a sound when it dawned on me because Gamble spoke again. "Trent? What is it?"

"We went to dinner last night," I said, then hastily explained, "Before Andi."

"Obviously, I know you weren't out after your daughter needed you." He confirmed.

"Right before we left the diner, Drew mentioned retiring. It was brief. We left so we could talk about it in private."

"Well, someone heard and decided it was their chance at a payday," he surmised.

I sipped my coffee without bothering to add creamer. I

needed the jolt of caffeine right about then. "I'll have Drew call you after we deal with the police."

"Take care of the kids first." Gamble agreed. "We'll have this wrapped up before Travis's birthday party this weekend."

My stomach tightened a little thinking about the party. So much had happened since last night. I hoped adding a party wouldn't be too much.

"I bought him a car."

Coffee spewed from my mouth and rained over the counter. "W-what?"

"It's his birthday."

"You can't just buy him a car."

"Why not?" He wondered. "It's a grandfather's right."

Drew's and my biological fathers might not be around, but our kids didn't lack for family. Between Gamble, Romeo's parents, and Braeden's mother and stepfather, Andi and Travis had three sets of "grandparents."

No one went by blood around here. Not even Rome's mom, Valerie. That woman was a kid hoarder.

"We, ah…" I began, rubbing the back of my neck. "We already got him one."

I mean, technically, we hadn't called or gone to pick it up. But… details.

"What kind?"

I told him.

"Does it even have an engine?" he asked.

"That's part of the fun. Rebuilding it with him."

Gamble made a noise. "Well, he can drive this one while he rebuilds the other one with you."

"I don't—"

"It's a done deal."

I sighed. "What kind of car is it?"

"A Black Diamond Bronco."

I set down the coffee. No point in trying to drink it during this conversation. "You're telling Drew," I said.

"It's a Ford. He'll be fine." When I didn't say anything, he went on. "Listen, I'm going to go. Check in and make sure those PIs are doing their jobs. I expect results. Call me if anything happens, and I'll do the same."

"Thank you," I said sincerely.

"It's too early for that," he replied gruffly. "Take care of those kids. Drew too."

Just then, Drew walked around the corner, hair a mess and expression disgruntled. I opened my arm, and he made a beeline for me.

"I will," I promised Gamble.

He hung up without a goodbye, and I set aside the phone so I could wrap both arms around Drew.

"Who was that?" he asked.

"Gamble."

He groaned.

"You want some coffee?"

He grunted.

Laughing, I turned toward the pot, and he went with me, clinging to my body as though he wasn't almost as big as me. I patted his head and then poured more coffee in my mug, then shuffled to the fridge for the creamer. Once it was added, I held it in front of Drew's face like a bribe.

He lifted his head but kept his arms around me.

I shook my head, holding it so he could take a sip. Only then did he pull back and take the mug for himself.

"Thanks, frat boy."

"Anything for you, baby."

"I'm assuming if Gamble was calling this early, there's drama."

I grimaced.

"Family all good?" he asked.

"Yeah."

He nodded and grabbed my wrist, towing me to the couch where he pushed me down and climbed into my lap. "Good. Let me drink this coffee in peace before shit hits the fan."

9

Drew

You know one thing I'm not going to miss when I retire?

The fucking headlines.

People are nosy pieces of crap, you know that? Who the hell takes a video of an eleven-year-old girl getting harassed and then almost kidnapped instead of helping?

Pieces of crap, that's who.

And even worse, media outlets trying to paint an almost-seventeen-year-old boy as a villain because he tackled the person trying to steal his sister. I don't give a damn if it was a woman. Someone had to stop her, and everyone else was too busy taking notes for headlines and payouts to do anything.

If any of those kids got hurt during that ice cream debacle, I'd be suing everyone. I could do it. I had connections.

Thankfully, the kids weren't hurt. At least physically. Mentally was a whole other story.

"Calm down," T murmured, using his large hands to

massage the tense muscles in my shoulders. "The kids are with us, and everything is under control."

"You think Lolo had nightmares last night?" I worried, thinking of Andi still asleep in our bed with Ketchup.

Trent reached around and tugged the phone from my grip, clearing all the asinine headlines I was staring at to pull up Romeo's number. He continued massaging my neck with one hand while waiting for Romeo to pick up.

A moment later, I heard his muffled voice.

"How's Lolo this morning?" Trent got right to it. "She have any trouble sleeping last night?"

I heard him answer but couldn't make out what he said.

Trent cursed quietly, and my stomach dropped because I knew that meant my niece had a night just like my daughter.

"Yeah, Andi too," Trent replied. Then, "I know."

Romeo said something else, and Trent made a sound. "Is she? Yeah, count us in. Okay, yeah. See you then."

Trent ended the call and tossed the phone beside him on the couch.

I started to turn, but both his hands landed on my shoulders and started massaging again. I groaned and hung my head.

"Lolo didn't sleep well either," Trent said. "After we talk to the cops, they're taking her down to one of Rim's shelters to pick out a puppy."

"Braeden is going to love that," I mused.

"It will give her something else to focus on. Puppies make everything better. At least according to Rimmel."

"You told Romeo we'd go," I said knowingly.

"Yeah." He was slightly sheepish.

"How the hell are you so calm right now?" I wondered, my voice going husky when he squeezed a particularly tight spot at the base of my neck.

"Oh, I'm pissed," he refuted.

"You're planning a trip to get a puppy and giving me a massage."

He went silent for a moment, but his hands never stopped.

God, his hands are fucking magic. Everything about him was.

"Staying calm for you and the kids makes me feel better."

Classic T. Focusing on all of us instead of himself. Some might call him sacrificial, but in truth, it was survival. Survival through service. Trent didn't sacrifice his own needs for others. He focused on others because it was what he needed.

You ever heard the saying *givers need to have limits because takers rarely do*?

Loving a man like this was tricky because it would be so easy to fall into a taker role.

Trent's heart had no limits. He would give and give until he had nothing left, and it was my job to make sure I filled him back up so he was never empty.

Turning from my seat between his legs, I rose to my knees, wrapped my arms around his waist, and bulldozed him back into the couch cushions, pinning him beneath me.

Bending my head, I mouthed his dick through his sweats, smiling a little at the way he purred. Grabbing the hem of his T-shirt, I lifted to push my head under it and kiss his stomach. The muscles there contracted with his sudden laughter, the burst of sound loosening the tightness in my chest.

Just because I could, I nipped at his defined abs and then traced the contours of his six-pack with my tongue. His laughter smoothed into a low moan, and I stretched up to tug his nipple into my mouth.

His back arched slightly, and my breath turned the small space between his chest and shirt warm. Releasing his nipple, I pressed a kiss to his chest just above his heart.

"You take good care of us, frat boy. I want to take care of you too."

"You do, baby. Better than anyone."

"Daddy?" Andi's voice made me jerk, the seams of T's shirt cracking a little with the force.

"Fuck," I muttered, remembering I was tangled in his clothes.

"I'm here, peanut," Trent called as I tried to untangle myself.

"Uh, Dad," Andi said, her voice closer than before. "What are you doing?"

I yanked free, cheeks hot, hair wild, and caught in the act. "Uh, what?"

Trent laughed.

The dirty bastard.

"What are you doing, Dad?" Andi asked, her dark eyes on me.

I glanced at Trent for help.

He raised his brow, waiting to see what I'd say.

Forget what I said about his need to help others. He clearly also enjoyed watching me suffer.

"Uh, well, your dad said something on his side was itching him, so I was checking it out."

"Oh. Do you have a bug bite, Daddy?" Andi said, turning those innocent eyes to Trent.

Trent glanced at me. "Did you find a bug bite, Daddy?"

"Sure did," I said, straight-faced. "Nothing serious, though. Just try not to itch it."

"Might be hard. It's pretty itchy," Trent said, his eyes full of laughter.

"Well, I'm not scratching any itch you have," I muttered and stood from the floor. Turning to our daughter, I said, "How about some breakfast, peanut?"

"Can I have apple cider?" she asked. "I know it won't be as good as Aunt Rimmel's, but I still want some."

"Sure," I told her. "I'll get the water on."

Trent pushed off the couch and bent down in front of Andi, tugging on the end of her long hair. "How you doing this morning?"

She shrugged. "Okay."

Instead of putting the water on, I sank beside Trent. "It's okay if you're still upset. You can tell us anything, you know that, right?"

"I'm scared to talk to the police," she said, tugging the bear in her hand against her chest. "What if they're mad at me?"

"Why would they be mad at you?" Trent asked.

"Because I caused a scene and spilled my ice cream. Trav got mad and tackled that lady."

"You didn't do anything wrong," I said firmly. "And neither did Travis or London."

Trent picked up where I left off. "What happened isn't your fault. The police know that. They aren't mad. They just need to ask you a few questions."

"What kind of questions?" she asked.

"What that lady said to you. If she seemed mad," Trent replied.

"She said she was my mom and you took me from her," Andi said. "But it was a lie."

"Lying is wrong. That's why the police need to hear what she said. They're trying to find her so she can't bother you again."

"Will she go to jail?"

I made a sound, and Trent gave me a look. I bit back the *if I don't send her to hell first!* reply about to roll off my tongue.

"She might," Trent reasoned. "But that's for the police to

decide. And if she does, it isn't because she lied. Lying is wrong, but you don't always go to jail for that."

"She tried to kidnap me," Andi said. "Is that why?"

Trent nodded. "Yeah. That's definitely something people go to jail for."

"She was scary."

Trent pushed into a standing position and plucked her off her feet. Andi's arms went around his neck to hug him, the bear hanging between his shoulder blades.

A lump formed in my throat seeing them like that. It never got old seeing him with our kids, and I knew it probably never would.

"I'm sorry you had to go through that, baby girl," Trent murmured, rubbing her back. "We're gonna make sure she doesn't scare you again. That's why it's important we talk to the police. Do you think you can do that?"

"Will you and Daddy be there?" she asked.

"We'll be there," I told her.

"Me too," Travis said, stepping off the stairs and walking into the room.

Andi nodded against Trent's shoulder.

"Okay."

"After we're done, we're going to the shelter with Aunt Rimmel and London."

Gasping, Andi pulled back to swivel and look at me. "Can I get a kitten?"

"I thought you wanted a puppy," Trent said.

"But we already have Ketchup. I've never had a cat before. They're so small and cuddly."

"Do you remember Murphy?" I asked, thinking of my sister's late one-eyed cat.

Andi nodded. "His picture is still on the mantel. Aunt Rimmel loved him a lot."

Travis made a sound and went into the kitchen to stand

in front of the fridge with the door wide open. *Tell me you don't pay the bills without telling me.*

"Cats shit in a box," he announced.

"Seriously, Travis?" I warned. "Your mouth is worse than any litter box."

He made another sound.

"Travis," Trent said quietly.

Travis pushed the fridge closed and turned. "Sorry," he apologized. Then, "What I meant was cats use the bathroom in a box."

Andi raised her hand. "I'll clean it."

"Like h—" Both T and I fired a look at him, and his lips pressed together. After a second, he tried again. "I'm not letting my sister clean up poop with a plastic shovel. I'll do it."

I held in a laugh. Every man in this house was wrapped around her cute little finger.

Andi's face lit up. "Really?"

Travis sighed, turned back to the fridge, and opened the door.

"Same thing was in there the last time you looked," I told him.

"So can I?" Andi asked. "Pleeease?"

Trent smiled. "As long as you give it a better name than Ketchup."

"Hey, that's a good name." I defended.

Andi squealed and patted Trent for him to put her down. "I'll go get dressed!"

"Thought you wanted apple cider!" I called after her.

"I do," she yelled back.

I shook my head and went into the kitchen to put water on to boil.

Trent wrapped himself around me from behind, and I turned my face to kiss him on the cheek. "You're a good dad,"

I told him quietly.

Ketchup raced into the room, slid over the tile, and knocked into his water bowl. Water sloshed all over the floor and on the baseboard of the island. He just kept right on going over to the back door where he barked.

Travis abandoned his extensive study of the inside of the fridge and went to let him outside.

Trent pulled away from me to push the door shut and point toward the island when Trav came back. "Sit," he ordered. "I'll make eggs."

"Bacon?" Our son was hopeful.

"And toast," Trent confirmed.

I poured a fresh cup of coffee, added a little creamer, and plucked the egg out of T's hand to replace it with the mug. "I'll crack. You whisk."

"I'll eat," Travis put in.

"That's really generous, Trav," Trent replied. "Thank you, son."

He grinned, and I snorted. "We're so thankful that we'll make sure to buy you the best pooper scooper we can find."

He groaned, and Ketchup whined at the back door. Travis let him in and then grabbed the carton of orange juice out of the fridge and sat down at the island with it. He didn't even get a glass, just started chugging.

Meh, one less dish to wash.

"Ugh, Trav, you're so gross," Andi said as she walked into the kitchen wearing a pair of jeans and a pink hoodie.

Ketchup danced around her feet, knocked into me, and I knocked into Trent. Setting aside his coffee, he stepped behind me, caging me in with his chest and arms, chin resting on my shoulder as I finished cracking eggs into a bowl.

"What are you doing, frat boy?"

"Eggs are expensive these days, baby. I'm just making sure you don't drop any."

"Gross," Travis muttered, swiping his chin with his sleeve.

Guess what color it was.

If you said black, you clearly have been paying attention.

"Good boy!" Andi crooned, and Ketchup raced out of the kitchen with a treat hanging from his mouth. He couldn't eat it on the floor like a normal dog. No. He had to jump onto the couch and enjoy it there.

What we created here together, in this house, was my favorite. Powerful enough to hit pause on the outside world and any challenges out there waiting. I hoped the kids felt it and knew we would always be here, no matter what.

THE INTERVIEW WITH THE POLICE WENT SMOOTHLY, AND THE girls didn't cry, which was a win in my book. Travis answered all their questions and didn't cuss once. Another win in the book of parenting. Andi sat in my lap, Travis right beside me, and Trent stood over us like the guard dog Lorhaven always claimed he was. Romeo did the same with Rimmel and London, and Romeo's dad tried to soften their glowering with a smile. It might have worked if Braeden wasn't also in the room.

We kept the rest of the kids out of it, even if I did suspect the little eavesdroppers stood at the top of the stairs and listened.

They asked Travis and the girls for a physical description of the woman and let us know afterward that it matched the description other witnesses gave. They also had the damn recordings all the bystanders took instead of helping. If you ask me, they didn't need to ask our kids what she looked like because they had her on video, but I guess they had to do their due diligence.

The uniforms seemed confident they'd be able to find her. I almost told them our PIs would find her first, but I wasn't about to be an asshole. I wanted all hands on deck when it came to getting this woman off the streets.

Knowing she was still out there, doing who knew what, made me want to keep the kids inside the security of the compound walls, but promises were made to two girls.

And so here we were, about to get our animal adoption on. The stone exterior of Rimmel's animal shelter was familiar as ever. The landscaping around it had filled in over the years. The bushes were full, flowers lined the walkway, and the climbing roses covered the entire corner of the front side.

The window boxes were empty, but the dirt was fresh.

"I'm going to be filling them for fall in just a couple weeks," Rimmel said as we approached. "And since Romeo is retired, he'll have time to help me this year."

"I'm all yours, smalls," he said, linking their hands.

"Can I help too?" Andi asked.

"Of course!" Rimmel replied. "The other two shelters need some flowers too. I need all the help I can get."

She still ran three shelters and was hands-on with all of them.

A car turned into the parking lot, and I tensed immediately, turning to stare down the approaching SUV. A man was driving, a woman in the passenger seat. I looked hard at the woman, trying to see if she matched the description of the one from yesterday.

Trent's hand settled over the back of my neck, giving it a reassuring squeeze. "It's not her," he said low.

I nodded once but scanned the rest of the lot and the main road beyond. The press was probably lurking.

"Come on, Dad!" Andi yelled.

I turned to see her waving at us from the door.

"Coming," I called back, and she raced inside without waiting. I glanced at Trent. "She could be anywhere," I told him from the side of my mouth. "What if she tries again?"

"Nothing is going to happen," T promised, voice like steel. "I won't let that nutjob anywhere near our daughter or son."

An intrusive thought blew through my brain like a scarf on a windy day, the potency of it halting me in my tracks.

Trent stopped when I did, concern written all over his face. "Drew?"

I swallowed, appalled at my own brain.

Trent filled my line of vision, hands cupping my face. "Tell me." His voice was gruff.

I glanced around, looking for the kids.

"They're already inside with Romeo and Rimmel," T said.

Nodding, I met his stare and wet my lips. Then I shook my head.

"Drew."

"I don't want to say it out loud," I whispered. "It's terrible."

"You can say anything to me."

"I-I…" I stuttered. "It was just a thought. One I don't mean."

Ever patient, Trent stroked my cheekbone with the pad of his thumb.

"I thought, *I'm glad she's dead,*" I whispered, looking at him in horror. "I didn't even mean to think that."

Trent made a sound and pulled me in, hugging me right there on the sidewalk. "You're a father who's worried," he said softly, not a trace of condemnation in his tone. "You just want them to be safe. I think what you really mean is that you're glad she isn't a threat to their safety. She can't come back and cause turmoil and confusion in their lives."

"I don't want to share them," I whispered. "Only with you."

"You're a good dad, Drew. It's just a hard day."

His words were comforting and made me feel less like an asshole.

Trent held me another moment and then stepped back. "We better get inside before Andi decides she wants one of everything."

"Especially since you lack the ability to tell her no," I teased.

"As if you're any better at it," he retorted, settling his palm at the small of my back and leading me inside.

"Touché."

"Maybe we should have brought Braeden," Trent mused.

The lobby of the shelter was clean and slightly scented of disinfectant. The summer intern sitting behind the counter waved as soon as we walked in. "They went that way," she said, pointing toward the area where the dogs were housed.

"Thanks," I replied.

"How ya doing, Kelsey?" Trent greeted. "Summer's almost over. Classes start up soon, don't they?"

She smiled slightly, and her cheeks turned pink. "Hey, Trent. Yeah, week after next," she replied.

"We'll miss seeing you around here. Thanks for helping our sister out this summer."

"Oh, Rimmel said I could stay on and help a few days a week this semester. So I won't be leaving."

"Oh yeah? That's great news."

Kelsey blushed even more, and I slid my arm through Trent's, linking us together.

A door burst open, and Andi appeared. "Dad! Come see Lolo's new puppy!"

"She picked one already?" I mused.

"It was love at first sight, Dad! Geez."

"Yeah, *geez*," Trent repeated.

I gave him a look. "That intern totally has the hots for you."

He threw his head back and laughed. "Are you jealous?"

"No," I growled.

I was totally jealous.

Trent's laugh quieted, and he leaned close. "You're the only one I want."

"Look!" Andi exclaimed and held out her arms like she was presenting a million dollars.

London sat on the floor with a golden puppy in her lap and three others all around her. Her long dark hair was wavy and mussed as though she'd been rolling around on the floor with four dogs—which, yeah, she probably was.

Purple-framed glasses bordered blue eyes that sparkled with happiness as the dog licked her cheek. She laughed and scratched behind the puppy's ear.

Another puppy climbed onto her lap, and she giggled more, scooping them both into her arms. "Daddy, look! They both want to come home with me."

I turned to where Romeo stood not far away, hands tucked into the Wolves jacket he was wearing, staring at his daughter with a wistful expression on his face.

"Dad," London called again.

He blinked and smiled. "You look just like your mother."

"Acts like her too," I noted, watching the puppies climb all over her.

Andi sat down and held out her arms. Two puppies rushed her, and she fell back with a squeal while they climbed all over her, tails wagging.

Laughing, Rimmel reached down to pet one and ended up on the floor with both the girls.

Trent, Rome, and I stood there shaking our heads at the

pile they made, but none of us hurried them along. It was good to see them smiling and carefree after everything.

"You know, when they asked for puppies, I didn't expect actual puppies. You don't get a lot of those here, do you, sis?" I asked.

Pushing her hair off her face, Rimmel sat up with one wiggling in her arms. The hoodie she wore was covered in dog hair, and there was drool on her glasses. "Not a lot. We do usually get animals that are a bit older, but these guys were left near the firehouse in town in a box. One of the guys brought them over the other morning."

"Kelsey posted them this morning, and we've already gotten a few calls, so I'm sure they will all have good homes in just a few days."

"What about the other dogs?" Lolo asked, looking toward the hall where the other dogs were housed.

"We'll find them homes too," Rimmel promised. "But sometimes the older dogs don't get picked as fast as the puppies."

"Why not?" Andi asked.

"Well, because they're older, and a lot of people want puppies because they're very cute."

"Grown-up dogs are cute too," Andi said. "Just look at Ketchup."

"Ketchup is definitely cute." I agreed.

"That name, though," Romeo muttered.

Trent made a sound of agreement.

Rude.

Lolo suddenly stood and handed the puppy in her arms off to her mother, then went down the hall.

"Strawberry, where you going?" Romeo called.

London looked over her shoulder. "To pick an older dog. I don't want them to feel left out."

Romeo turned his eyes to his wife. "She's killing me, smalls."

Rimmel sniffled and pushed to her feet, nearly pitching sideways when the puppy in her arms started wiggling to get down. I grabbed her arms to steady her, and she smiled, sheepish. "Thanks. You mind?" she asked, pushing the dog into my chest.

I couldn't exactly say no, so I tucked her into my chest. A wide, wet tongue dragged along my chin and up to my lower lip.

"Ack," I said, turning my face.

The puppy's tail beat against my stomach.

"She likes you, Dad!" Andi said.

"This one is a troublemaker," Trent declared and pointed to one tugging on his shoelaces and growling like it was vicious.

A few minutes later, London, Romeo, and Rimmel appeared from the hall with a dog trotting along beside London.

"This is Sampson," she told us, laying her hand on his head, which was about hip high to her. He was all black with a patch of white on his chest and nose. He had short hair, but it somehow looked wild. "He's three years old, and he's coming home with us."

Sampson looked up at her like she hung the moon and stars, and when she leaned down to hug him, he licked her nose.

"You sure he's the one you want?" Romeo asked.

London gasped and put her hands over the dog's ears. "Dad! You'll hurt his feelings." She pulled her hands away. "Of course he is! Just look at him! He's the most handsome dog ever!"

Andi ran over and patted his head. He licked her too.

"Who wants to help me wrangle these puppies back into their condo?"

Rimmel called all the rooms the dogs stayed in "condos." She said it was nicer than calling them cages or kennels.

Once they were secured, Andi raced to the other end of the shelter where the cat condos were, and we watched her greet all five that were there.

"That one is hiding, Aunt Rimmel," Andi said, pointing through the glass at one of the condos in the back.

Rimmel nodded. "She's very shy. She doesn't come out much. I think this place is a little noisy for her."

"Can I go in there?" Andi asked.

"Sure," Rimmel said. "But don't be sad if she won't come out. Some animals just need space."

After punching in the code, the door swung open, and Andi stepped inside the small room. I moved closer to watch through the glass, and Trent did the same.

Andi walked to the back of the condo and sat down, stretching her legs out in front of her. After a minute, she called to the cat softly.

Nothing happened at first, and I glanced at Trent, worried Andi was going to be disappointed. But then T made a soft sound and gestured for me to look. I turned in time to see a small white cat with black paws and a black ear slowly approach my daughter. Andi rubbed her fingers together, and the cat hesitated before going right to her and rubbing against her hand.

Andi looked at Rimmel, excitement spilling over in her eyes, and Rimmel gave her a thumbs-up.

A few seconds later, the cat climbed onto Andi's legs, sat down, and looked up at my dark-haired baby girl.

Andi smiled and started stroking its head and back. The cat started to purr so loudly that Andi giggled.

"She looks like a panda," Andi said, looking up at me and Trent.

"You're right. She does." Trent agreed.

"She's so little. How old is Panda, Aunt Rimmel?"

Rimmel checked the paperwork at the door. "Panda is female and approximately nine months old. She was found on the side of a road, and we think she was probably born in the wild."

"That must have been scary," Andi said, still stroking the cat. "You can come live with me. My brother looks scary, but he's not."

I laughed under my breath.

Andi looked up. "Dads, can Panda come home with us?"

Even if Braeden had been here shouting, *Oh, hells no!*, no one would have listened.

So yeah, everyone, meet the newest members of the fam: Panda and Sampson.

10

Trent

Travis sleeps with his bedroom door closed. He didn't when he was little, but probably about two years ago, he started closing it when he played video games late at night and didn't want to bother his little sister.

He probably hoped we would think he was sleeping too, but we ain't fools. Even so, the tradition continued, and now I think he just liked his own space.

The closed door was the perfect opportunity for birthday shenanigans.

Shenanigans, as in Drew and me staying up late to hang caution tape across his door, securing it on each side of the frame. It crisscrossed and zigzagged from floor to ceiling, making it look like a bona fide crime scene. Once the caution tape was up, we blew up *a lot* of balloons—a mix of black and hot pink—and stuffed them between the tape and the door.

We were lucky he slept with AirPods in his ears because the noise we made wasn't exactly nonexistent. And also...

when did blowing up a massive pile of balloons get to be so hard?

I mean, sure, Drew had gray hair and was talking retirement, but me? I was a spring chicken.

Once that was done, we set up a camera in the hallway and angled it to the door, you know, to send to the fam later.

Trav's seventeenth birthday dawned, and we huddled in the hallway, drinking coffee and waiting for him to wake up. I knew he wouldn't sleep half the day away because our entire fam was here for his party.

Down the hall, a bedroom door opened, and Arrow's dark head peeked out. Even years after he'd buzzed all the blond off his head and let it grow in to his natural shade of brown, I was still sometimes surprised when I saw him. I guess he'd be a bleach-blond kid to me forever.

Seeing Drew and me, he lifted his chin. "He awake yet?" he whispered.

We shook our heads.

The bedroom door opened farther, and Hopper appeared, wearing nothing but a pair of sweats. Arrow took one look at him and pointed into the room. Hopper smirked like he knew exactly what he did and sauntered out of frame as if he were proud of himself.

Farther down the hall, another door opened, and Joey came out with Lorhaven towering behind her.

Joey's dark hair was the longest I'd ever seen it, hanging almost to her waist, and she was wearing a pair of silky-looking pajama pants with a matching button-up top.

"Is he awake?" Joey whispered.

"No," Arrow whisper-yelled back.

Jagger ducked under Lorhaven's arm and stepped out into the hallway, looking at all of us before shaking his head. Pulling his phone from his pajama pants, he hit the screen, and seconds later, a muffled ringing burst from behind Trav's door.

The ringing cut off, and Jagger said, "Just get up already."

After tucking the phone back into his pocket, he rolled his eyes. "You guys are so lame."

"Andi," Trent called toward our daughter's room, and seconds later, she bounded out, hair floating around her. Sophie came out behind her, and both girls waited impatiently.

Travis's door handle rattled, and I smacked T in the stomach to get his attention.

It rattled again.

Whoosh. His door pulled open, and all the balloons between him and the caution tape tumbled in, raining over him in a wave of black and neon pink.

"What the f—"

"HAPPY BIRTHDAY!" yelled everyone crowding the hallway.

Andi pulled out a confetti popper and pointed it at him.

"Andi, don't even—" *Pop!* Multicolored confetti exploded out of the tube and blasted Travis and the balloons piled around his feet.

He folded his arms over his chest and scowled as sparkly confetti clung to his black clothing and the caution tape holding him hostage.

"Is this what you two kept whispering about all day yesterday?" Travis asked, glaring at Drew and me.

"It's not every day our son turns seventeen," I said, basically agreeing even though this was definitely not what we were whispering about.

He shot us all an unamused look and then swiped the tape still draped across his door free with a swing of his arm.

Balloons bounced and rolled into the hallway when he

stepped forward, and I grabbed him by the shoulder to pull him into a hug. "Happy birthday, son," I said against his ear.

"Thanks, Dad."

I pulled back, and Drew moved in, embracing him in his iconic hug. When Drew pulled back, Travis saw his aunt and uncles waiting and let out a groan.

Joey laughed and wrapped her arms around him anyway. "Happy birthday, Trav. We love you," she said, swaying back and forth.

"Thanks, Aunt Joey."

Lorhaven offered him his fist, and then Hopper did the same. Arrow hugged him.

"Can I have some coffee now?" he asked.

"Yes, please," Sophie echoed.

I gestured for them to go downstairs, and they went instantly with Jagger and Andi hot on their heels.

"What is it with kids and coffee these days?" Lorhaven wanted to know.

"They drink it because it's trendy," Drew muttered. "We drink it for survival. We are not the same."

"More balloons!" Andi exclaimed from downstairs, and Drew and I shared a smile.

When we all walked into the open kitchen, Trav turned from the island, a slight flush to his cheeks. He glanced at me, then away. Then to Drew and away. "You didn't need to do this."

We'd been decorating for his birthday since he became ours. We did the same for Andi. Every year, we set up the island with balloons, a cake, candy, streamers, and anything else we picked up so it was the first thing they saw when they came downstairs.

"We wanted to," Drew told him as he walked to the coffeemaker to brew a fresh pot. Sophie was already at the

Nespresso machine making herself a latte, and he tugged on her dark ponytail, making her laugh.

Sophie favored Lorhaven with her facial structure and cheekbones. Her eyes were hazel like a mix of Joey's green and Lorhaven's dark. At nearly sixteen, she was already five feet seven, and her hair was made up of wild ringlets like her mom's.

Jagger had wide green eyes and a mop of curls. He was still young yet, but judging from the size of his feet, dude was gonna be tall.

"It's tradition." I reminded Travis.

He huffed. "I'm not a kid anymore."

"No, but you'll always be our son."

Andi punctuated that with another explosion of confetti, which blasted over the island and onto everyone standing nearby, mostly her brother.

"Seriously." Trav sighed, brushing the shiny flecks off his black shirt. "Where are you hiding those?"

"I'll never tell."

The front door swung open, and Rimmel stepped in, partially hidden by a stack of presents covered in bows. "Happy birthday," she sang.

Ketchup rushed her, and the pile of gifts toppled onto the floor, revealing her wide-eyed expression.

"Cleanup crew on aisle Rimmel!" Braeden called, coming inside. His hands were filled with boxes of donuts.

Blue, Asher, and Jax all rushed in to pick up the scattered boxes while Romeo picked up his wife. "I told you not to carry all that."

"You aren't the boss of me," she retorted.

The boys piled the gifts on the island, sending loose confetti everywhere.

"Did we already miss the party?" Ivy asked, propping her hands on her hips to stare at the mess. Her blond hair was in loose waves around her shoulders, and she was dressed in a pair of wide-leg jeans and some sort of vest with oversized gold buttons.

"No, you're just in time," Drew said from behind the counter.

After hugs and more birthday greetings for Travis, all the kids plopped onto the sectional in the living room to stare at their phones.

Seriously, how are almost all of them teenagers already?

Andi carried Panda around to show her to everyone—and everyone pretended they hadn't seen her yesterday—and Lolo went behind her to introduce Sampson.

"The caterers will be here at three," Ivy told me as I got to work cracking eggs for a breakfast casserole. We were gonna have to make at least two of them to feed everyone.

Because it was such an undertaking to feed all of us, we hired out catering for Trav's party. No one wanted to be in the kitchen because this was family time.

"We'll meet them at the gate and bring the food in," Drew said. "I don't want them on the property."

Yeah, usually hiring a caterer made things easier… but today, it seemed to be just the opposite.

Ivy slid a worried glance to me, and I lowered my voice. "We thought we would have found her by now," I said of the woman who'd tried to kidnap Andi. "The longer it drags on, the more worried we get."

Understanding filled her face. Laying her hand on my shoulder, she turned to Braeden. "Go with Drew later to get the food. Take the truck."

B nodded. "Will do. Me and Rome can man the grill later too."

"I'll be on standby with the fire extinguisher," Lorhaven cracked.

"Har-har, Lor. It was one tiny fire," Braeden retorted.

Lorhaven smirked. "Good to see your eyebrow grew back in."

Braeden rubbed his eyebrow, almost checking to make sure it was still there. "A man singes his eyebrow one time."

Everyone laughed.

"What can I do to help?" Joey asked.

"Balloons are being delivered too," Rimmel said. "Maybe you can help me bring those down."

Arrow stepped forward. "Me and Hopp will do that."

Joey turned, giving her brother a look. "You think we can't handle some balloons?"

"Rim would probably float away with them," Braeden muttered.

Rimmel gasped. "I would not!"

"Your organizational skills are needed to organize the food and table, baby," Romeo said.

Sighing, Rimmel looked at Joey. "That's mansplaining for they don't want us around a bunch of strangers at the gate."

"They have a point," Lorhaven added.

Beside me, Ivy straightened. "There's a lot of stuff to do anyway since the caterers won't be setting up. We can't let them do it." She nodded toward the guys. "They wouldn't know how to style a charcuterie board even if we showed them a picture."

"I know it goes in my belly," Romeo cracked.

"Get in my belly!" Arrow chanted.

Hopper snagged a blueberry donut from a box and shoved it into his mouth.

"Hey," he said, pointing to the mouthful jammed between his lips. "That's my favfrite."

"Thanks," I said quietly to my sister while everyone else laughed.

"You're welcome." She took the whisk from my hand. "If you beat those eggs any more, they're going to coagulate."

My nose wrinkled. "Do eggs do that?"

"I don't care to find out."

Laughing, I went to grab the sausage and cheese while she added the eggs to two large glass dishes.

A short while later, a birthday breakfast was served, family style. And then it was party time.

"I SHOULD GO INTRODUCE MYSELF," BRAEDEN ANNOUNCED, staring down the kid currently walking right beside Nova.

"He's one of your football players." I reminded him. "Pretty sure you've met."

Braeden pursed his lips, and we all looked back to see the kid say something and Nova laugh. Her long hair floated out around her, and her cheeks glowed a little pink.

The kid seemed happy with the reaction, and he leaned in to nudge her with his shoulder.

"Obviously, he doesn't know me well enough," Braeden growled and started forward.

Romeo caught him by the hood and towed him back. "Hold on there, Hulk."

Nova's giggle floated over from where the pair sat on a bench near the fire pit with his arm draped causally over her shoulder.

"Oh, hells no," Romeo said, letting go of B so the pair of them could stalk their way over.

Drew and I shared a look and then went after them.

"If you ever want to see the field from somewhere other than the bench, you'd better move that arm, Falls," Braeden intoned.

His arm was removed immediately. "Sorry, Coach."

"Sorry for getting caught," Romeo said, and B nodded.

"Mr. Anderson, sir," the kid squeaked.

Drew and I stepped up, and he put his hands under his thighs.

Nova let out a loud sigh. "Seriously?"

"Introduce us to your date, midge," Drew said, pinning those baby blues on him. I'm thinking this guy didn't find them as appealing as me.

"Do not call me that," Nova hissed. Pushing to her feet, she glanced beside her. "Come on, Jordan. Let's go get some food."

Jordan swallowed and stood but hesitated at the wall of men in front of him.

I took pity on him and offered my hand. "What's up, man? I'm Nova's uncle, Trent."

He shook my hand. His palm was only a little sweaty.

I made sure to squeeze tight. "You make sure to treat my niece right."

"Uncle Trent," she whined.

I smiled nice and wide at him. "I'll be sure to watch you during your next game."

"Thanks," the kid mumbled.

"What is going on over here?" Ivy called as she and Rimmel approached.

"Introducing ourselves to Nova's friend," Romeo said.

Ivy made a noise. "Why don't you two go get some food? And there's a dunk booth over there that your Uncle Arrow just sat in."

Nova and her date rushed away.

"There ain't no kissing booth here!" Braeden yelled after them.

Nova glared daggers over her shoulder.

"What in the hell is wrong with you?" Ivy said, taking all four of us in with one disgusted look.

"Just being hospitable, princess," Romeo said, flashing a white smile.

"That charm doesn't work on me, Romeo." Ivy sniffed.

"Just letting the kid know we got eyes on him," Braeden said, pointing to his eyes.

Ivy stepped close, her average height and frame dwarfed by Braeden, but she didn't back down. Jamming a finger into his chest, she said, "If you've scared that boy off from taking her to a movie later, you're sleeping on the couch for a month."

He scoffed.

"Do *not* mess with me, Braeden James."

He grimaced. "But, baby—"

"Oh, look," I said, seeing the black SUV coming down the road. "Gamble's here."

"Sorry, sis," Drew was quick to say. "We gotta go greet him."

All four of us took off, with her calling a warning behind us.

"You'd think she'd be thankful we were watching that hornball," Braeden muttered.

"We're just gonna have to be quieter about it," Romeo surmised.

"I gave his hand a good squeeze," I added.

"Good one," B congratulated.

"I'll hack his social media and sneak around," Drew offered.

"Now this is the kind of brotherly love I need," B drawled.

Gamble was getting out of the back seat when we walked up. "Why do you four look like you're going to need my lawyers?"

"Us?" Drew asked. "We're angels."

"Lucifer was once an angel," he deadpanned.

"We were just introducing ourselves to Nova's date."

Gamble's eyes gleamed. "Date, you say? I'll need his name for a background check."

"I wish my wife were more like a man," B said. Then he made a face. "Actually, no. I don't."

"I'll introduce you to him later," Romeo said, shaking his hand. "How are you, Ron?"

"Anderson. Retirement looks good on you."

"It would probably look good on you too," he suggested.

Gamble made a rude noise. "I'll retire when I'm dead." His eyes moved to my husband. "Guess you don't have the same work ethic."

Drew laughed. "Not everyone is made of steel like you."

"I give you two years, tops, before you're at my door asking for a job."

Drew chuckled. "You'd give me one."

"Well, I can't have you working for my competition."

"Do you have competition?" Braeden wondered.

"No."

"We're glad you could make it," I said around a laugh. "Got a bottle of scotch and a steak waiting for you."

"You know the way to a man's heart."

"He's taken," Drew said, making me look his way. When he winked, I considered dragging him into a room with a lock on the door.

"Keep your dick in your pants, Mask. I want to see my grandkids."

"Right this way," I said, leading him toward the sprawling deck off the back of the main house.

"Oh," he said, stopping to look at me and Drew. "I've got Travis's birthday present up on a truck at the gate. Wasn't sure where you wanted it."

"A truck?" Braeden wondered. "You had to have it trucked in?"

"It's a Bronco," I told him.

Romeo whistled.

"My birthday is next month," Braeden told him.

"Buy your own car," Gamble shot back. Turning to Drew, he said, "You got your panties out of the wad they were in over this?"

Drew sighed. "It isn't that I'm not grateful. I just want you to know we don't expect this kind of stuff."

"I know." Gamble was gruff. "But if I can't spend my money on my family, what's the point of having it?"

Abruptly, Drew leaned in and hugged him. Gamble stiffened a little in surprise, but Drew didn't let go. If anything, he hugged him tighter.

Romeo and B gestured to the party, and I waved them off.

"Thank you," Drew said, still hugging the man. "Not for the car. But for being there for our kids."

Gamble made a sound and reached around to pat his back. "It's been my pleasure."

Drew pulled away and glanced at me, and I gave him a reassuring nod.

"I knew you'd be good parents from the first moment I saw you with those kids, and I'm never wrong."

"You're also very humble," Drew noted.

"Being humble is like hiding a diamond in a sock drawer," he declared. "Now, about the car…"

Hiding my snicker, I answered, "I'll go let them through the gate in a few."

"Good. Now, about *GearShark*," he said, moving right along. I couldn't help but wonder what it was like inside his brain. "You'll meet them in two days."

Wait, what? "Two days?" I echoed, glancing at Drew. He seemed just as clueless as me.

"They wanted to meet tomorrow. Always were afraid of being scooped," he said as we headed toward the deck. "But I told them you needed time to fly over to Gamble Speedway."

"Gamble Speedway?" Drew echoed.

Ron made an impatient sound. "As if you two didn't know

there'd be a *GearShark* interview. There's *always* a *GearShark* interview."

"What exactly is this interview for?" I asked.

"Drew's retirement, of course. Every media outlet is scrambling and sending offers for the exclusive."

Surprised, Drew looked at me. "Is that true?"

I grimaced. "To be honest, I haven't checked the emails this week. I was too focused on Trav's birthday and trying to find that woman."

"Your priorities are where they should be," Gamble butted in. "That's why my office has been fielding the offers."

"And I guess you chose one too?" Drew mused.

"Don't be stupid."

I laughed.

"Gamble Speedway. Two days. It goes without saying, but I'm going to say it anyway because you two aren't the brightest in the bunch."

Should I be insulted?

"Do not talk to any other press. This is an exclusive, and they are paying you very well for it."

Drew hesitated.

"What now? You don't like money?"

"I'm just not sure if it's a good time," he replied.

"Did you change your mind about retiring?"

"No." He was succinct.

Gamble made a rude sound. "So it's about that wack-adoodle giving everyone the slip."

"We thought she'd be in custody by now," I told him. "We can't keep them on lockdown forever. School starts soon."

I gazed across the yard to the kids all gathered around the dunk tank we'd set up. Arrow was sitting inside, already soaked, while Travis picked up a football to throw at the target. Andi said something, and he held out the ball and she took it, putting her back into the throw.

It fell short and hit the ground. Arrow cheered that he got to stay above water.

Travis picked her up and ran at the tank, stopping in front of the button.

"Cheater!" Arrow hollered so loud I heard him where I was, and Andi's laugh burst into the wind when she slammed her hand down on it and Arrow went under.

"We have to protect her." Turning back to them, I said, "I'll do whatever I have to in order to protect them."

Gamble nodded. "As will I. I'll make a few calls. Light an inferno under some asses."

I knew everyone was doing everything they could, but it just wasn't enough.

"And you can bring them with. I'll send my plane for you. My house is secure. You can stay with me," Gamble added.

"What do you think, T?" Drew asked, and I met his unsure gaze.

I thought it over and nodded. "Okay. As long as you're ready to announce your retirement."

"I'm ready." Drew was certain.

"Then in two days, we'll make it *GearShark* official."

11

Drew

We might have been a little cautious about having this party with a nutjob still on the loose, but as I stood there in the midst of our family laughing, smiling, and stuffing their faces (mostly Arrow), I couldn't deny that being with family is *never* a bad idea.

I also couldn't help but wonder how the hell I had a seventeen-year-old son.

Like, what? I might have a few grays, but I still had a lot of miles left on these tires. Even if they were changing direction.

A seventeen-year-old *and* retirement.

This year was shaping up to be a banger. It didn't feel like an end, though, or a clock winding down. If anything, I felt invigorated by the possibilities ahead. I wasn't sure what I wanted to do yet, which side street I would turn onto. For once, I wasn't speeding somewhere but was willing to check out the scenery instead of flying by it.

Maybe I'd take Gamble up on a job at the NRR. Maybe I'd become a coach or a sponsor. Maybe I'd go back to something with computers—nah, probably not. The office and tie gig was not the life for me.

Maybe I'd become a stay-at-home dad and bake pies. I was already an expert at reindeer food.

Hell, I could buy a diner and serve up the best fries in town.

Now *that* had some possibilities.

From track master to fry master. Hells yeah.

Trent broke away from Arrow and Hopper and started toward me. His jeans were well-worn and molded around his thighs, the edge of the pocket near his hip frayed, loose strings waving as he walked. The hem of the open vintage Adidas jacket Ivy had come home with one day fluttered back to reveal the thick white T-shirt molded against his waist.

Forget what I said about all those possibilities. They were nothing at all compared to the certainty of him.

Noting the way I practically ate him with my eyes, his darkened, the lines at the corners deepening. He paused long enough to set down the plastic cup in his hand, the air between us crackling with chemistry as his palms slid over the sides of my waist to envelop my back.

"You keep looking at me like that and we'll never make it to the cake," he said in a shiver-inducing tone.

Gliding my palms upward over his pecs, I looped my arms around his neck and laid my forehead against his. "Then stop walking around like that."

He arched a brow. "Like what?"

"More enticing than a French fry."

His eyes did that crinkle thing again, and my stomach swooped. "That's high praise from a fry monster like you."

"You gonna kiss me or what?"

"Oh… I'm… gonna," he murmured, lips brushing mine with every syllable before settling completely.

Humming in appreciation, I tangled my fingers in the short strands of hair at the base of his skull, tugging him that much tighter against me. T moaned, the sound vibrating my tongue, and I swallowed it down, letting it echo into my belly.

His tongue tasted like punch and mine like beer, two flavors that did not go together but were suddenly my new favorite combo. Trent's hands slid from my back to my ass, tucking into the pockets on my jeans. He gave a whole new meaning to that saying *pocket full of sunshine.*

A high-pitched whistle interfered with my good time, and Trent chuckled into the kiss. When he retreated, I growled and tried to pull him back, but he just grabbed my hands and kissed them quickly, eyes dancing with happiness. "I am one lucky bastard."

I shook my head once, forcing the words through a hoarse throat. "I'm the lucky one."

"Who's the one-upper now?" he mused.

Romeo appeared, slapping Trent on the back. "The driver is on his way down from the gate," he said.

My addled mind cleared, and I glanced over my shoulder, but the truck wasn't in sight yet. "Now?"

"If we waited until you were done making out, the car would be rusted over," Romeo drawled.

Trent twisted around. "I thought Lorhaven was escorting him down."

"He's already up there," Romeo mused. "He texted to say they were coming."

Trent nodded. "I'll gather everyone up."

Romeo's teeth flashed. "B already did that."

Upon our surprised looks, Romeo pointed toward the

entire fam, which had already gathered around Braeden. I guess he was the one who'd whistled.

Romeo leaned in to tease Trent. "Maybe we should call *you* Romeo."

Trent pushed his head away. "Oh, fuck off, Rome. You know you and Rimmel are just as bad."

Laughing, he threw an arm around each of our shoulders, squeezing his big-ass frame in the middle. "Does this make me the filling in a Trent and Drew sandwich?" he wondered as we walked toward the group.

"Dude. You hang out with Braeden too much," I told him, pushing his arm off me and then shoving it off Trent. He could get his own man.

Romeo cackled as Lorhaven's Corvette crested the hill. It was an old model like the one he'd totaled in a race way back in the day.

T and I went to the front of the group where Trav was standing beside Gamble.

"What's going on?" he asked the second he saw us.

"Grampy here got you a bougie birthday gift," I wise-cracked.

"Call me Grampy again and see what happens," Gamble retorted.

The flatbed truck appeared, a single black SUV clearly on the back.

Travis straightened, eyes following the truck like it was raining money. "Are you serious?" he asked, wide eyes flying to Trent and then me.

I nodded. "Maybe you should ask your *grandfather*."

Ripping his eyes off the approaching vehicles, Travis turned to Gamble. "Grandad?"

Gamble's lips turned up a little at the corners, his eyes warming. "Figured I'd get you a car since your dads never have."

"We just want him to be ready," I muttered.

"He's ready," Gamble announced. Laying his hand on Trav's shoulder, he said, "It's not a race car, but it's loaded and big enough to haul your football gear and a few friends."

Lorhaven pulled off into the grass and parked while the truck slowed to a stop a few feet away.

"Holy shit, is that a Bronco?" Blue exclaimed.

"Language!" all the adults admonished.

"It's a Black Diamond Bronco," Gamble confirmed.

The driver got out of the cab and walked toward the back to unload the SUV. Travis stood there speechless.

"Well, go on. Go tell me if you like it."

All the kids ran toward it, staring at it from beside the lowering flatbed.

"It's awesome!" Jax yelled.

"Look at those rims!" Jagger put in.

Lorhaven laughed.

I mean, it was pretty decent for a non-race car. A good choice for driving around with his sister, I guess.

And it was a Ford.

Travis jogged back, stopping in front of Gamble. "You really got that for me?"

"Hm." He agreed. "But you gotta keep your grades up. And no getting in trouble. Just because I gave it to you doesn't mean your dads can't take it away."

Travis plowed into Gamble, the older man rocking back on his heels. Trent and I moved to jump forward, afraid they were going down, but Gamble waved us off.

"Thank you, Grandad," Travis said against his shoulder. "I promise I'll take care of it."

"I know you will." He was gruff. "You're a good kid. You deserve it."

Damn. Did some pollen just blow in? Maybe some

ragweed? We needed to get a gardener out here pronto because suddenly my allergies were wild.

Trent grabbed the back of my neck, and I turned to look at him through blurred vision. T smiled and swiped beneath my eyes.

"Damn allergies," I muttered.

"Grampy! I want a pink one when I turn seventeen!" Andi called.

I let out a cross between a laugh and a sob while everyone snickered.

"I'll put it on order, sweet pea," Gamble told her but then turned to me, eyes narrowed. "Look what you started."

"You can always tell her not to call you that," Trent advised.

Gamble made a rude sound. "I'll just learn to live with it."

I barked a laugh. "The great and powerful Gamble finally bested by an eleven-year-old."

Gamble gave me a look that would make fresh paint peel and then turned away. Trent winked at me behind his back.

"I saw that," he groused. Then, "Travis, what are you waiting for? Go look at the engine. I know you want to." He tossed Trav a key fob and shooed him off.

Trav turned to go but then stopped, hesitated, and turned back. His eyes locked on me, and I tilted my head. "What's up, Trav?"

"Do you want to come check it out with me?"

Damn ragweed. Nodding, I cleared my throat. "Ah, yeah. Of course."

Travis turned to Trent. "You too, Dad?"

He nodded, and we started after our son. T glanced at me. "I think I need some allergy medicine."

Listen, don't laugh at us. Our son wanting us to be part of his big moment was special.

"That should do it," the man unloading the Bronco said as we approached.

"Thank you," Trent said, holding out his hand to shake. "Appreciate you bringing it all the way out here."

"Just doing my job," he said, making sure everything on the flatbed was in place. "If you wouldn't mind moving it off to the side, I'll just go up there and turn around and head out."

"How about we take it for a spin?" I asked Travis.

"Yeah!"

"I'll escort him off the property," Trent said.

"No." Lorhaven jumped into the conversation. "I got it. You go with them," he said, gesturing to me and our son.

"You sure?"

"Crystal."

"Josie, want to go for a ride?" Lorhaven called to his wife.

"Yes!" she exclaimed, jogging toward the Corvette.

Lorhaven grinned at us. "Looks like I got me a date."

"Just make sure you do it off the street. There's kids here," I cracked.

He smirked. "You didn't seem to mind two minutes ago when you were sucking face with—" The sound of Travis gagging cut off his words.

"I'll make sure he gets off the property and the gate is latched." Lorhaven redirected.

"Would you mind checking in with security out there too?" Trent asked, voice much lower than before.

"Will do," Lorhaven replied just as quietly before jogging over to the Corvette.

The large flatbed started up, the rumbling engine loud.

I glanced around for Andi. She was with London and Sophie, throwing water balloons at the boys. "Peanut, you wanna go for a ride?"

"She's soaking wet!" Travis complained. "Think of the interior."

Spoken like a true gearhead.

"Later," Andi yelled, launching a balloon at Asher.

"We'll be right back," I called.

Rimmel waved and nodded because Andi was already back to her game.

The flatbed and the Corvette headed off down the paved road between the main house and our house so it could turn around, and we went toward the new Bronco.

It was pretty sweet, with a glossy black finish, matte black removable top, and custom lift kit to accommodate the thirty-five-inch all-terrain tires that were upgraded with a set of rims I was pretty sure weren't supposed to hit the market until spring. The word BRONCO was blacked out across the grill between the round headlights, and the rock sliders on the sides were heavy-duty.

Gamble obviously had impeccable taste.

"The door isn't latched," Travis said, pointing to the driver's door. He was right. It wasn't fully latched.

"The guy who unloaded it probably didn't shut it all the way," I said, going over to peer in the windows. The interior was all black too. "I call shotgun!" I hollered, running around the back as Trav climbed into the driver's seat.

Trent was already there, holding the passenger door open for me. "As if I'd ever dream of taking shotgun," he teased.

I grinned and slid in past him, making sure to brush the front of his jeans on the way. His chuckle cut off when he shut the door and slid into the back.

"I can't believe you let him get me a car," Travis said, hands gripping the steering wheel as he gazed around in awe.

"No one lets Gamble do anything," Trent said from the back seat.

"Yeah, so make sure you call him Grampy a few times just to drive him crazy," I said.

Travis clicked the seatbelt into place and started it up. "If we upgrade the intake and exhaust, it will sound even better."

Did I mention I really loved this kid?

"Better get rolling before Lorhaven and the flatbed come back up." Trent reminded him.

Travis took off down the road, excitement pouring off him in waves. I gazed around the interior, snooped through the glove box, and noted the heavy-duty floor mats.

"Here they come," Trav said, and I looked through the windshield to see the truck and Vette coming up the road.

"Good thing she's got big tires," I said, and Travis cut the wheel, going off-road and up through the grass.

"This is fire!" Travis said. "Seriously. No cap."

For us oldies, that just meant he really liked it. Like seriously.

I looked it up on that click-clock app they all love so much.

"How's it handling?" Trent asked from the back seat. "Make sure you give yourself time to learn how it drives."

"I know, Dad. Cars are like women. Every one of them is unique."

Feeling my eyebrows shoot up, I leaned around the front seat to look at my husband. "Did you teach him that?"

"I thought you did," Trent replied.

I pursed my lips and turned back.

"You been talking to Lorhaven?"

Travis laughed.

That was a yes.

"Don't worry. It applies to men too."

"How diverse of you, son," I remarked.

"Diversity is a fact. Inclusion is a choice." Travis flicked a glance in the rearview. "Right, Dad?"

Now that was *definitely* something my husband would teach him.

"You got the rizz," Trent called.

Travis made a sound. "Don't ever say that again."

I peered into the back once more. Trent shrugged. "I learned it on the Tok."

After a short drive, Trav turned it around and went back to the party. We still had a cake to cut. And a nineteen seventy Mach 1 waiting to be revealed.

"You like it?" I asked when he put it in park near Lorhaven's Corvette.

"Are you kidding? It's the GOAT."

"Well, don't tell Uncle Romeo that because he's under the impression he's the GOAT," Trent joked. Then, "Make sure you tell Gamble thank you again."

"I will." Travis agreed and then hesitated to get out. "Dad?"

"Yeah?" I answered, knowing he was talking to me.

He rotated in the seat, eyes meeting mine. "Are you sure you're okay with this?"

Trent seemed to melt into the shadows of the back seat, also knowing this was a question for me.

"Yes, I'm one hundred percent okay with this," I confirmed. "We know how much you wanted a car of your own."

He nodded. "Yeah. I can give it back if you don't—"

"I don't want you to give it back. I want you to drive it. Make it yours. We…" I went on, including Trent. "Know you're ready."

Any reservation that Travis had blew away like dust behind a tire on a dirt road. He smiled and hugged me fast before yelling, "Thanks, Dads!" and jumping out of the car. "*Dudes*," he said to Blue, Jax, Asher, and Jagger as they all came jogging over.

Trent laughed under his breath and got out, opening the passenger door for me. "That went well."

"The GOAT," I muttered. "Just wait 'til he sees the inside of our garage."

Trent threw his head back and laughed. "Don't be jealous, baby. He will love your car more."

"It's our car." I reminded him. "It's from both of us."

He shut the door, and we stepped around the hood of the Bronco when Rimmel came running over, her face white as a ghost.

"Rim?" Trent said, rushing toward her. "What's the matter?"

"I can't find Andi," she said, voice high and breathless.

"What?" I asked, hair on the back of my neck standing straight up.

Rimmel shook her head. "She was just there playing with the other kids. And then suddenly, the girls were calling for her, and now no one can find her."

"Okay, well, she couldn't have gotten far. Maybe she went down to the house to check on Panda," Trent said, a strong voice of reason as I looked around frantically for a flash of her dark hair.

Rimmel's eyes filled with hope. "You think?"

"Yeah, she wanted to bring her up to the party, but I told her to leave her at home," T said. "I'll go down there right now."

My heart was pounding, ears ringing as clammy sweat coated my palms. *Trent's right. She probably went to check on that damn cat. She's fine.*

And then a very distinctive scream pierced the late-afternoon air.

Andi.

12

Trent

I'm a guy who tries not to think the worst. I try to stay positive and especially to be strong and calm for my family.

But hearing Andi scream like that? Not knowing why or where she was?

Strength splintered. Calm succumbed to chaos.

In that moment, my eyes sought Drew, and when they found his panicked blue stare, I remembered my reason. My true strength. It didn't matter how splintered I was or if a cyclone of chaos brought me to my knees. I would crawl if I had to, brandishing my splintered insides as weapons.

No one messed with my family. *Oh, hells no.*

Heart pounding, I started running, pulling out my cell as I went. I hoped it was a good sign that the scream came from the direction of our house. Maybe she had gone to check on the cat. Maybe she just fell on the way.

But why didn't she tell anyone? If she was hurt, why didn't she call?

"Andi!" Drew yelled, keeping pace beside me. "Andi!"

The absence of her answer rang loud in my ears and caused the panic to snowball inside me. The second it loaded, I checked the location tracking on her phone, clinging to that pulsing red dot like a lifeline. "She's over by the garage," I yelled, picking up my pace.

I was aware of shouting and pounding footsteps in step with mine, but I didn't take my eyes off the place I was going. The only face I wanted to see just then was hers.

It didn't matter that I had a location and was just with her twenty minutes ago. It didn't matter that we were at home on our family compound. The bad feeling worming through my veins was overwhelming, shoving back all rational thought. Somehow, someway, even with all the precautions we'd taken… somehow that woman had gotten to my daughter. I knew it deep down in my bones.

The bright-pink object lying abandoned in the grass forced a pained grunt out of me as I snatched it off the ground, turning it over to find the screen cracked.

Lurching to a stop beside me, Drew stared at our daughter's phone. "It's her." He panted. "How the fuck did she get on this property?"

"Andi!" I roared. "Andi, where are you?"

It was echoed about ten times by various members of the family doing the same.

I strained to hear past the whirring between my ears and the thick anxiety attempting to hijack my thoughts.

The garage doors were down. The front door of the house was closed. *The side door!*

I sprinted around the large free-standing garage where the side door was wide open, and I lunged forward, bursting inside.

"Andi! Andi Mask, answer me right now," I yelled, my voice echoing in the massive space. The flimsy cover hiding the Mustang we'd gotten for Travis fluttered lightly from the disturbed air, but nothing else moved. Nothing made a single sound.

"Trent!" Drew yelled from outside, and I tore back out into the yard, heart in my throat. "Look." He pointed to the separate shed a short distance from the garage. It was shaped like a mini barn with a black metal roof. The side door to that was open as well.

We shared a brief look and started forward together, but the sound of an engine turning over stuttered my steps. I didn't even have time enough to wonder if what I heard was what I thought it was because the engine turned over again.

Someone was trying to start one of the four-wheelers.

What. The. Fuck?

I started forward again just as the large garage-style door on the front of the shed began sliding up, the sound of the motor drowned out by a four-wheeler firing to life.

"Andi!" Drew yelled, racing through the open side door just as the ATV lurched forward from too much gas.

I held my breath as it barely cleared the still-rising door and bounced over the ground, the back end fishtailing a bit from another burst of the throttle. The mad woman driving pitched sideways in her seat, hair blowing back to expose her maniacal expression.

And there was my daughter. My peanut.

Strapped to the back of that mechanical bucking beast and fighting to stay on.

Time stopped for an extended second, and during that brief pause, our eyes connected. Her terror was palpable. The cords in her neck stood out from the force of her shout, the sound muted because of the gag stuffed into her mouth.

"Jump off!" Drew yelled, running through the shed toward her, and Andi thrashed her head from side to side, lifting her bound hands as if to say, *I can't, Daddy!*

Bound and gagged right under my nose.

Rage dropped a veil over my vision, tinting everything with the vivid shade of blood. An unholy growl ripped out of me, the sound so menacing the woman trying to kidnap my daughter—*again*—looked up.

Our eyes clashed, and whatever she saw in mine rattled her so deeply that she flinched, hold slipping off the hand grips and making the quad stall.

Drew reached Andi, pulling her off the back and into his arms. Realizing she'd never get out of there with my daughter, the woman frantically restarted the four-wheeler, clearly planning to escape.

Over my cold, dead body.

The quad shot forward, and I ran at her. A mean glint flared in her eyes, and she jerked the handlebars to speed directly at me.

Everyone started yelling and waving their hands. I knew they wanted me to move.

Again I say, over my cold, dead body. Like hell I'd let this woman escape. This was ending. Today.

I started to run, essentially right into a game of chicken with a psycho on a four-wheeler. Smirking, she leaned forward, and my body readied for impact, bending slightly at the waist. It happened fast. My shoulder slammed into the handlebars as my arm shot out in a clothesline move, knocking her out of the seat.

We collided and went down, both of us rolling across the ground before skidding to a stop. Pain shot through my shoulder, and a loud crash filled the air behind me, but I ignored both because the woman scrambled up and started to run.

I tackled her into the grass, pinning her facedown.

She fought despite me being twice her size, back arching

and chin jutting up toward the sky. "She's mine! *Mine!* You can't have her!"

I reached around, slapping a hand over her mouth, and she bit down on my finger with a wild grunt. I felt my skin tear, and I cursed beneath my breath but refused to let go. Her words were poison, and I'd bleed to keep them from my kids' ears.

Her screams and bucking continued, and for a moment, I truly wondered if maybe she was mentally ill. But then I heard my daughter crying, and any compassion I might have had went up in smoke.

Jamming my knee between her shoulder blades, I braced my hand beside her head and leaned down. "This is over. You will *never* get near my kids again."

13

Drew

Turned out she'd been squatting in the woods about a mile from our compound. The police found her "campground," which was essentially a few ratty blankets under a tree and a bag filled with magazine articles about us and our kids.

It was why no one could find her. She'd been literally in the middle of nowhere… close but not close enough that our security team noticed.

She had no identification but was later confirmed to be Irene W. Coleman. No one knew what the W stood for, but I could take a few guesses. None of them would be nice. The only reason she was identified was that an institution on the other side of the state recognized her (from the news) and called the police. She'd been a long-term patient there, then rehabilitated and released.

She'd only been out for six months. Three months ago, she stopped checking in with the outpatient therapist.

Three months ago was also when the letters started coming.

We assumed she saw the photos of Andi and Travis and became fixated. I have no idea how she got across the state or why it was my kids she latched on to. I was just glad she was back in custody and getting the help she clearly needed.

Even knowing some of the details and understanding this woman clearly needed medication and supervision, I was still angry. How could I not be? These were my kids.

Oh, and if you're wondering how she got onto our property… She climbed into Trav's new Bronco while it was parked on the flatbed outside the gate. She must have hidden on the floorboards and gotten out when no one was looking. That also explained why the driver's side was unlatched when Travis went to get in.

With the threat to our kids' safety no longer in play and the police interviews concluded, things were finally quieting back down on the compound. All the kids were piling into the home theater for a family movie night with buckets of popcorn and too much candy.

"Trav," I called, catching his eye from the recliner he was sprawled in and jerking my head in the direction of the door where Trent leaned in the frame.

It really should be illegal to be that sexy.

As if he knew my thoughts, he smirked, a promise of later glimmering in his hazel eyes.

"What's going on?" Travis asked when he met us by the door.

"We never got to give you your birthday present," Trent said, straightening off the jamb. If the massive bruise covering his shoulder from when he used himself as a human battering ram ached—like I knew it must have—he didn't show it.

My heart stopped when I saw him challenge that four-wheeler. I'd managed to cover our daughter's eyes, but I couldn't force mine away. God, the risk he took. I understood why. Hell, I would have done it myself if I hadn't been holding Andi. But I was, and all I could do was watch him put himself in harm's way.

Thank fuck he was okay. That they all were.

Travis's brows drew down. "You threw me a party. Plus, the cake, balloons, and you got me that black jacket I wanted."

I scoffed. "That wasn't your present."

"It wasn't?"

"Nope," Trent replied, popping the P.

"What is it?" Travis asked, looking between us.

I grinned, excitement making my stomach flutter. "How about we go find out?"

"Now? I thought we were watching a movie."

"They're going to argue over what to watch for at least thirty minutes," Trent mused.

It was true. No one could ever pick.

"Okay."

"Go ahead," Trent told us. "I'll catch up."

Trent went to tell our daughter (and everyone else) where we were headed and caught up to us on the back deck just as we started down the stairs.

The sun drooped heavy in the evening sky, its fiery streaks piercing through the rustling trees and making the horizon bleed gold and crimson. Our shadows stretched in front of us as we made our way across the grass to our house, three elongated forms in a line, the two on the ends a little wider and longer than the one in the middle.

Autumn hummed in the air while summer hushed completely as everything around us held its breath for the final moments of day before being claimed by night. I felt the precipice deeper tonight because I, too, was transitioning to a new season. Years ago, that would have scared me, adrenaline being almost an addiction and something I couldn't really imagine myself without. But now, here, on the night before I told the world I was stepping away from racing, fear was the furthest thing from my mind.

I was too wrapped up in contentment to feel the pull of adrenaline because it was no longer my drug.

"Where are we going?" Travis asked as our footsteps crunched over grass. "Why didn't you just bring it up to the main house?"

Trent shot me a smile.

"It's not something we can just carry around," I replied.

"If it's some kind of gold pooper scooper for that cat, I'm going to crash out."

Trent guffawed.

"What does that even mean?" I wondered.

Travis shrugged. He probably didn't know either.

Trent caught Trav's hood when he started up the stairs to the front door. "Wrong way," he said, tugging him back.

Travis gave us a look. "You're being weird."

I directed him to the last door at the end of the garage. "Stand here," I said as we took up either side of him.

Trent pulled a remote out of his pocket. "Ready?"

Travis sighed.

The door started rolling up, revealing inch by inch of the Mustang draped in heavy cloth. Even after the door stopped, Travis stayed where he was, barely moving. Just staring.

"Well?" I said, too excited to wait.

"What is that?" he asked.

"Why don't you go find out?" Trent goaded.

He swallowed so hard his Adam's apple bobbed. Tucking his hands in his pockets, he looked at me, then at Trent. "Is that what I think it is?"

"Depends. What do you think it is?" I asked.

"A car," he half whispered. It almost sounded like a prayer.

Butterflies erupted wildly beneath my ribcage, making me feel slightly nauseous.

"Gamble already bought you a car." Trent reminded him.

"Not that kind of car," Trav said, stare fixed on the cloth.

"What kind then?" Trent asked.

He whispered. "The only kind that matters."

A sudden flash of the little boy with too-small clothes and a toy Mustang clutched in his hand overwhelmed me, and tears crowded the back of my eyes. Seriously, there were so many that it was an impending tsunami.

Family isn't always something you're born into. Sometimes it's something you find.

Thank God I found him.

"Why don't you go look?" Trent encouraged him.

Travis jogged forward, stopping in front of the car to stare before moving to the side and bunching the cover in his hands.

"Thank you, T," I whispered, voice as wet as my eyes. "Thank you."

I felt his head turn in my direction. I felt his enveloping stare. "For what?"

"For my son," I replied, finally turning so our eyes could collide. "For this family. For not just being my best friend but my everything."

With the sky ablaze behind him, the outline of his shape burned with shades of glimmering gold and rouge, making him appear exactly what he was: my heart on fire.

"Dad!" Trav's voice pulled me around even though I was still captured by the spell Trent cast on me. "Come on!"

I heard the words but didn't really process them until Trent's warm palm settled between my shoulder blades and slid up to grasp the back of my neck. "He wants you to help him."

Just like that, day succumbed to night, and the moment I'd been savoring offered more.

"Go on," Trent shooed. "Go show your son his new toy."

I started away and then swung back, leaping into his arms and drawing out a hefty *ungh* from his lungs. "*Our* son." I corrected him before leaping back down and jogging over to the opposite side of the hood.

"Ready?" Travis called.

"Go!" Trent hollered.

We pulled off the massive cloth with me tugging the excess to my side so the car revealed itself to Trav first.

"*No fucking way!*" His disbelief pierced the night, causing ripples in the quiet but the very best kind.

Trent chuckled under his breath, and my heart felt like it was trying to claw its way out of my chest.

"Are you for real?" He went on, stepping back and rubbing a hand over the lower part of his face. "No fucking way."

Neither of us bothered to correct his language.

"What do you think?" Trent called as he came closer.

"It's a nineteen seventy Ford Mustang Mach 1. What do you think I think?" Travis said, pacing in front of it and then going around to look at the side.

"It's black," he said almost to himself.

"Like your soul," I cracked.

"He's got some glitter in there too," Trent mused. "Andi made sure of that."

"It needs new tires," Travis said. "Headlights, coilover suspension," he listed and rushed past us to pop the hood to look at where the engine *should* be. "And a new engine."

Only a true gearhead would be happy to receive a car with no engine.

"Needs a fuel injection too," I added.

Travis nodded thoughtfully. "A new paint job too, probably." Dropping the hood back in place, he dragged the pads of his fingers across the hood. "It has different styling than yours."

I nodded. "Mine's a year older."

Trav nodded as though he already knew that because, yeah, he did.

His sneakers squeaked against the garage floor when he turned abruptly to face us. "This is seriously mine?"

Trent nodded. "All yours if you're willing to put in the work to restore it."

Travis's genuine laugh was music to my ears. "That's half the fun!"

He wrenched open the passenger door, and it squealed so loud it sounded like a bad horror film. "Gonna need to fix that!" Trav said as if the idea excited him and crawled into the seat to check out every detail inside.

Laughing under his breath, Trent draped an arm over my shoulder, and we watched him through the dirty windshield. "These are original parts!" he exclaimed. "Oh, hells yes!"

"I think he likes it," I mused.

"That's an understatement."

Moments later, Travis was in front of us, cheeks flushed and eyes glittering like uncut diamonds. He looked high on life. High on adrenaline.

My legacy isn't what I'm leaving on the track. It's him.

"When can we start working on her?" he asked, then, "I'm going to make a list. I gotta go down to the—" He shook his head. "The shop here isn't gonna have what I want. Gonna have to drive down to Grandad's house. Maybe he'll let me order the parts through the guy he uses for the track."

"Slow your roll," I drawled. "This car isn't going to come together overnight."

"That's why I gotta start now!"

Trent laughed. "How about just get started on the list first?"

Travis nodded.

"So here's the deal," Trent said in a dad voice I've never quite been able to master. He just literally echoed with authority even without trying. "We will absolutely help you build this car, and when it's done, she's all yours. But you have to keep your grades up."

"I will," Travis promised, the fastest agreement for good grades he'd ever given.

"Don't be late for football practices. Stay out of trouble."

"I will, Dad. I swear."

"No street races."

He snorted. "In the Bronco?"

"Listen, that Bronco could probably beat half the cars your friends are driving," I told him.

He pursed his lips.

I held up my finger. "Don't even think about it. That's not why we let your grandfather give you that car."

"You just wanted to one-up him with this one," Travis cracked.

"That is not true," Trent said.

I snorted, and Travis laughed.

Trent was not amused. "The Bronco is a safe car for you to drive around to school and practices. That way you don't have to drive our SUV or my old Mustang."

At the mention, I glanced into the garage at the steel-colored Ford he'd been driving when we met. *Of course* we still had it. It was part of us.

"If we catch you racing—"

"You won't." Travis cut him off. "I swear. I'll drive how I'm supposed to." He shot a look at me. "Unless Dad is with me."

Listen, the kid had to get it out somehow. Might as well do it with me supervising.

Trent nodded. "Okay. And you can help Aunt Rimmel at the shelter on the weekends when you can. It will help pay for parts."

"And then we'll see about a job after football season is over."

Travis nodded. "Okay."

"That easy?" I mused, surprised there was no pushback at all.

"Are you kidding?"

"I guess this is the only kind of car that matters," Trent quipped.

Travis plowed into me. It was unexpected, and the breath whooshed from my lungs. "Thank you," he said, squeezing me tight. Damn, this kid was good at hugs. "Seriously, Dad, thank you so much."

I returned the hug, feeling that tsunami of emotion welling up inside me once more. "You're welcome, son. Happy birthday."

Travis pulled back as abruptly as he'd struck, but instead of going to thank T, he hesitated.

"Something on your mind, Trav?"

He nodded once but hesitated again, the bottom of his shoe scuffing the floor. "You aren't like him," he rushed out, looking anywhere but me.

His words were a boxing glove dead center to my chest. My heart skipped a beat, and the oxygen rushed from my system, leaving behind an achy, deflated feeling. "Ahh, what?" I rasped.

Sensing how unsteady I was, Trent stepped up behind me, his big body offering a place to lean.

Travis glanced back at me. "I know that's what you worry about. That you're going to fuck it all up like he did."

"You gotta stop saying fuck, Trav," Trent murmured, but it was only half-hearted.

"Like who?" I said, forgetting about the cursing.

Travis swallowed. "Your dad."

"What do you know about him?" I asked, not in a challenging way, just a curious one.

We didn't talk about my parents to our kids. We told them simply that they were people we didn't want in our lives. Travis once asked why, years ago, and we told him it was because they weren't very nice. Our kids didn't dwell on them or their absence because, frankly, they left no void to think about. Travis and Andi had an entire family that loved them. It was enough to make up for anyone who didn't.

"I know he was an asshole."

"Travis," Trent warned. "Watch your mouth. And don't talk about..." I practically heard his brain grind while trying to decide what to call them. "People like that."

"I read what he did to you," Travis said, looking straight at Trent. "How they made you stay away from Dad when he was in a coma. How they tried to keep you apart."

"Who told you that?" I asked, heart pounding harder.

Travis hesitated, eyes dropping to the floor. "I read it online."

Trent sighed. "Travis," he implored. "We told you not to read that crap. They just make stuff up to sell magazines."

"So it's not true?"

"You should have come to me if you had questions," he said, skirting the subject.

"Okay," Travis said and met Trent's stare. "Is it true? Did they really make you stay away from Dad?"

Trent's shoulders moved. "Yes."

"And they said terrible things to you?"

"Yes."

"Like when he told you Dad was dead?"

"What?" I roared, the reaction so visceral I knocked into

Trent. He caught me by the shoulders, but I twisted, staring at my husband. "Trent, is that true?"

Trent's eyes darkened with shadows, and I knew it was true. The scars from that time in our lives would always be inside him.

Trent didn't say anything, and I turned back to our son. "Where did you hear that?"

Travis seemed a little unsure, as if he'd uncovered some piece of ancient history that no one was supposed to know. "Uhh…"

"It's okay, Trav. Just tell me," I said.

"Some article. Some nurse they interviewed. They said Dad walked into your room, and you were gone. They heard someone tell him that you were gone."

A pained sound ripped out of Trent, and I spun, catching his face between my hands.

"T," I implored, searching the ghosts haunting him. "Is that true? Did he really tell you I was dead?"

"Just that you were gone. Gone and never coming back," Trent replied, voice hollow. "I assumed that's what it meant, and he didn't clarify…"

The rage I thought I'd gotten rid of years ago came back with startling force. I guess I was also covered in scars—this one just ripped open. "Why didn't you say anything?" I demanded, voice rough.

"Romeo came. He told me it wasn't true," Trent murmured.

"You should have told *me*."

Trent's eyes found mine, and I saw the same vulnerable expression he'd worn years ago. "Hearing it was enough. I'd rather cut out my tongue than repeat it even once."

"Oh, T," I groaned, wrapping my arms around him. No, wrapping my entire body around him. He hugged me back, his deep breaths brushing against my neck. "I'm sorry," I whispered. "So sorry."

Behind us, Travis cleared his throat. "I shouldn't have brought it up."

I pulled away from my husband to face our son. "You can bring up anything. You can talk to us about anything, anytime. It doesn't matter what it is. We will always be here for you, and we will always love you. No matter what."

"That's what I mean, though," Travis replied.

"What?" I wasn't following. Those fresh wounds from old scars were making it hard to think.

"You aren't like him. I know he disowned you for loving your best friend. For living the life you wanted and not the one he did."

"Is all this out in the media?" I wondered. Because goddamn. Trent and I didn't read the news after my accident. We were too busy putting our lives together and making a family with two kids.

Maybe I should have. I would have been prepared for our kids snooping.

"Well…" Travis hedged.

"Travis," Trent intoned.

"I might have asked Aunt Ivy."

I let out a choked sound. "You talked to your Aunt Ivy about this?"

"He's her dad too," Trav defended. "Figured she'd know better than the internet."

"Well, that's the truth." I agreed.

"Next time, ask us, okay? Anything you want to know," Trent said.

"But it hurts you."

"You being afraid to ask us something hurts way worse," Trent said candidly.

He always was better with words than me.

Travis nodded. "Okay. You won't ever be like him. I know you support me even if I do something you don't like or bring home a girl instead of a boy. I know that you made me wait for a car because you wanted to be safe, not because you were trying to hold me back."

"You're a smart kid, you know that?" I rasped, heart in a vise.

"Did you just come out as straight to us?" Trent asked.

I blinked.

"I hate to break it to you," Travis said sincerely, "but I like girls… a lot."

Trent nodded sagely. "We support you no matter who you love."

A laugh bubbled out of me. And then another.

Trent joined in, and pretty soon, all three of us were standing there laughing.

"You're a good dad. Both of you."

Travis's sincere words knocked all the humor out of me, and I sucked in a breath while blindly reaching behind me for Trent. When his hand closed around mine, I could finally breathe again. But then Travis kept talking.

"And I know that accident wrecked your lives, but it's the reason I have you, and I'm glad."

We rushed forward, squishing the kid between, hugging so hard he probably couldn't even breathe.

"That accident didn't wreck our lives, Travis," Trent told him. "It changed it. For the better because it brought us you and your sister. You two were worth every hardship, and you are the best thing to ever happen to us."

I hummed my agreement, getting all up in my feels. *Damn.*

"You're our son, Travis, and nothing is ever going to change that."

I felt him nod against us, and Trent lifted his head. When I looked up, he kissed me.

"Ew, okay. I'm done."

We pulled back, letting Travis breathe. His cheeks were red, as were his eyes. "Can I go look at my car now?"

I laughed. "Five minutes and then we have to go watch the movie."

He groaned.

Trent took my hand and led me out of the garage, just beyond the light spilling out of the open door. We blended into the shadows as he pushed me up against the wall.

"That was unexpected," he said quietly.

"There's something special about that kid, T."

"Yeah." He agreed. "There is."

"There's something special about you too."

Trent's white smile flashed in the dark. "Must run in the Mask family then because I could say the same thing about you."

"I don't need to be special, T. I just want to be happy."

"And are you, Mask? Are you happy?"

"Of course I am. I have you."

14

Trent

With the chaos in our rearview, Drew and I drove to Gamble Speedway, old-school road trip style.

It was a complete blast from the past with me riding shotgun, hand on the gearstick, while Drew drove too fast. We stopped at a roadside diner for greasy fries and listened to old songs too loud.

When we drove onto the speedway, the entire *GearShark* crew was already there in full set-up mode.

"You ready for this?" I asked as Drew parked.

He gazed out across the speedway and smiled. "I really am."

He seemed ready. Not an ounce of hesitation in the air.

"What about you, frat boy?" Drew asked, dimple making an appearance. "You ready to be married to a washed-up driver?"

"Washed-up?" I scoffed. Leaning in, I rubbed a hand over his scruff. "I prefer the term trophy husband."

He laughed.

"I got you something," I told him, reaching for the glove box.

"Pretty sure the blow job I got on the way here was enough."

"Close your eyes," I instructed.

"For real?"

"I went to a lot of trouble sneaking this in here, Mask. Close them."

"Fine, fine," Drew said, lashes fanning over his cheeks.

"No peeking," I instructed, reaching inside to pull it out.

"What is it?" Dude was so impatient.

I put it in my palm and held it in front of him. "Okay, you can look."

His eyes immediately flew wide and dropped to the item sitting on my hand.

His teeth flashed. "You already gave me one of these," he said, palming the magic eight ball.

"Yeah, well, that one was homophobic. Thought we could use a new one."

Drew laughed.

"Plus, this is a mini. You can put it in your pocket. If Emily asks you a question and you don't know, you can—"

"Ask the eight." He finished, repeating what I'd told him the first time I gave him one of these.

"Try it out," I encouraged.

Smiling, Drew closed his fingers around it and shook it up. "Will me and T be together forever?"

"Ooh, going right to the hard stuff."

He turned it over so the little triangle inside floated to the surface. After reading what it said, he looked up.

"Well?" I urged.

"Very likely."

"Look at that. It *is* all-knowing."

Drew shook his head. "Still lame as ever."

"That's why you love me."

"Thanks for the gift, frat boy."

"You're welcome, baby," I said, leaning in to kiss him. When I pulled back, I noted someone approaching the Mustang. "Here comes Emily."

Drew shook his head. "Couldn't even wait for us to get out of the damn car."

"I bet she was Sherlock Holmes in a past life," I joked.

"Nah, she's like that lady who wrote the gossip in the newspaper from that show our sisters made us watch."

I pursed my lips, trying to remember.

"You know, with the funny hats." Drew pointed to his head

"Ah," I said. "Lady Whistledown."

Ivy and Rimmel really loved that show *Bridgerton.* When the new season came out, they had a tea party theme for pancake Sunday.

It was ridiculous, but Andi loved it.

"Yeah, her." Drew agreed. "Serving tea to the ton."

"Don't worry. I won't tell the girls you secretly liked that show," I teased.

"Let's go before Emily tries to get in the car with us," he said, tucking his mini eight ball into the pocket of his leather jacket.

I didn't even have the door closed before Emily was on us. "Drew! Trent! It's been a while. So good to see you."

Emily Metcalf was a nice woman who'd worked at *Gear-Shark* for Drew's entire career. She'd broken a lot of stories and spun a lot of headlines over the years. Honestly, though, every time I saw her, I couldn't help but think about how she hit on Drew the first time they met. Was I a bit salty? Maybe. But Drew did love salt on his fries.

"Emily, you age like a fine wine," Drew said smoothly, giving her a brief hug when she leaned in.

I preferred beer over wine.

"Charming as ever," Emily purred, turning to me.

"Emily." I greeted her. "Good to see you," I said around another brief hug. "How have you been?"

"I've been great."

"Glad to hear it," I said genuinely.

"And you two? How have you been?" Emily asked. Drew started to answer, but Emily held up her hand, stopping him. "No. Wait. Save it for the interview."

"Ah, yes, everything we say can and will be on record," Drew quipped.

"Goes with the badge," she said, holding up her press pass.

"So tell me about today's shoot," I said. "I have to say I didn't expect such a big crew."

"As if we'd give our cover models any less."

Surprise shot through me. "Cover models?"

"Of course. Did you think we would have the most famous NRR driver and his handsome hubby as anything less than a cover story?"

"Well, I expected Drew to be on the cover..." My words trailed away.

"We want you both," Emily said directly.

"Like together?" Drew questioned.

"Of course. You're racing's hottest couple and have been for over a decade now. That deserves a couple cover."

"A couple cover," I repeated.

"Just picture it," a man carrying a camera interjected and gestured in front of him like he was painting a vision. "Blue skies, the sexy speedway as our backdrop, our award-winning racer in his fire suit, and his sexy, muscled hunk of a husband pulling him into his chest with the wind in their hair."

"Uh, who are you?" Drew asked, completely underwhelmed.

"David. David DaSilva," he replied. "I'm the visionary artist for today's shoot."

Drew looked at me.

"He's the photographer," I said simply.

"But it's so much more than a photograph," David said. "It's the details that matter most. The colors, the pose. And looking at you both, I can see it perfectly." He turned to Emily. "I want it to have an old-school bodice-ripper feel but like modern and sporty."

"Ooooh, love that," Emily cooed.

"A bodice-whatta?" I asked.

"No," Drew deadpanned.

David and Emily both looked at Drew as if they'd never heard the word no before. Which was obviously a lie. Drew told Emily no years ago. *Ahh, good times.*

"Ooh!" Emily gasped. "Celebrating a decade of #manlove. Racing's most-loved couple talks cars, raising a family, and keeping their #trewlove alive."

"It's a masterpiece!" David declared.

"Oh God, not the ship name," Drew muttered.

"Did our brother email you?" I asked.

"Which brother?" Emily asked.

"Never mind." She didn't need any more ideas.

"And of course we will be talking about those retirement rumors," Emily sang.

"It will be iconic." David decided. "Let's get you both into makeup and wardrobe."

"You know, I would love to, but I didn't bring my suit."

"Olivia!" David yelled.

A dark-haired woman appeared, carrying Drew's suit.

"Ron Gamble was kind enough to have it sent over," David said.

Clearly, no one had ever told him no before.

I laughed.

Drew gave me a look as though I'd betrayed him. It only made me laugh harder.

"Har-har, frat boy," he retorted. "We haven't seen your getup yet."

"Those jeans will do quite nicely," David said, circling around my body and making a sound of appreciation. "There's no need for a shirt."

"Oh, hells no!" Drew roared.

This just kept getting better.

"Well, why not?" David asked. "You married a snack. Why not brag about it?"

"T is not a snack. He's a whole meal."

"More like a buffet. One you just keep going back to," David said out of the side of his mouth. Emily giggled.

My lips rolled in.

"He's mine," Drew declared.

Ah, there he is. My possessive bastard.

"Don't be greedy," David admonished.

I stepped forward just as Drew did, intercepting him on his way to do bodily harm. Wrapping my arm around him, I spun us both.

"We're going to craft services to get a coffee," I called over my shoulder.

"Then straight to wardrobe!" Emily called. "We'll do the interview after the shoot!"

"Are they insane?" Drew bitched. "That man was practically drooling on your ass."

"I didn't notice."

A rude sound ripped from his throat. "You were practically bursting at the seams."

Unable to hold it anymore, I cackled. "You should have seen the look on your face."

"You need to stop working out," he groused. "We're old now. You don't need all those muscles."

"But, baby, I thought you liked my muscles," I bantered.

"I'd like them better if people stopped gawking at them."

"I only notice when you do."

He snorted. "Lying to your husband is a crime."

"Oh, look. They brought fries."

Drew perked up and looked to the display of fries. A fry-cuterie, if you will. It was actually really impressive. An entire wooden board covered with steak fries, crinkle cut, waffle, and even shoestring. All of them were golden and sprinkled with sea salt and garnished with parsley. Various dipping sauces in containers shaped like tires were nestled in the mounds of potato goodness, while small checkered flags on toothpicks decorated the entire board. And then, of course, in the center was a large bottle of Heinz ketchup.

"Is this heaven?" Drew asked.

How quickly he forgot about my muscles.

I watched with uncontained amusement as he descended on the fry-cuterie, filling both hands with fries.

"They're still warm." He moaned, shoving an impressively large waffle fry into his mouth.

I didn't bother to point out the heat lamp over the board. I'd just let him live his dream.

"I need ketchup," he said, turning up his nose at all the fancy dipping sauces. He even bypassed the cheese.

Laughing under my breath, I grabbed the bottle of ketchup, gave it a shake, and then dumped some beside the heaping mound of shoestring fries.

"I fucking love you, frat boy," Drew said, dunking three fries into the red sauce and jamming them into his mouth.

I patted his ass. "I know, baby."

I left him to his joy, made myself a coffee, and grabbed him a water.

"I thought that might butter him up," Emily said, sidling up to me.

"You were right."

"Think he'll do the shoot?"

"T!" Drew called. "There's curly fries too!"

I laughed. "I think he can be convinced."

Thirty minutes later, Drew was dressed in his red fire suit, and I was still in my jeans. I did exchange the T-shirt I'd been wearing for a blue button-up. Drew's hair was styled off his face, his blue eyes on full display. My hair was down over my forehead, not usually my normal style, but the girl in wardrobe said it made me look more mysterious. I didn't know what that meant, but I wasn't going to argue. Drew was already grumbling enough.

"Manlove," he griped as I stepped in front of the camera with him. "Braeden is going to have a field day."

"The race car is clashing with his suit!" David yelled from the sidelines. "It's ruining my vision!"

We both turned to look at Drew's car, which had been pulled onto set while we'd been changing.

"Clashing colors is not sexy!" David ranted.

The car was taken off set, and David had us get into place.

"It's missing something," he said, lowering the camera and gazing around. "That! Whose car is that?" He pointed at the Fastback.

"It's mine," Drew said.

"Yours?" David asked. "It's the perfect color! Bring it onto set!"

Drew gave me a look.

"Did I mention how sexy you look in that suit?" I asked.

Drew pulled the fastback into the background, and everyone adjusted the lighting and set to accommodate.

"Trent! Drew! In the front," David directed. "Yes!" he said

as we moved in. "Drew in the front. Trent, arms around him from behind."

The camera clicked, and then we changed positions.

"Sit on the hood," David told me. "Spread your legs."

Drew made a sound.

"Drew, get between them."

With a harumph, he moved between my knees.

"No. No. It's not the vibe," David said, lowering the camera. "It's missing something." He raised his hand, and Olivia, his very dedicated assistant, rushed over, and the pair exchanged a few short words. Olivia ran off and came back with a long, checkered scarf clutched in her hand.

She approached Drew, and he gave her a look.

"David wants to try this," she said, draping it around his neck, flinging one end over his shoulder.

"Yasss!" David called.

Olivia ran away, and Drew looked at me. "For shit's sake, T."

I laughed. "I've never seen you so stylish."

Drew gave me the finger.

"Trent, put your arms around Drew. Embrace him like you can't get enough."

"Well, that's easy," I mused, grabbing Drew around the waist and yanking him into me. "I definitely will never get enough of you."

"He's acting like this is for some romance novel at the grocery store," Drew griped.

"Aww, baby. Just smile and pretend you love me."

He sighed. "I don't have to pretend."

"Forget about them," I murmured, pulling him closer. "Just look at me."

"You are my favorite sight," he whispered.

His track suit was thick beneath my palm, and even

though it was clean, it was permanently scented with sweat and motor oil.

"I can't believe it's been ten years," I told him.

"It's been more than ten."

Just before our lips brushed, David interrupted. "Take off your shirt, Trent."

Drew jolted back. "What?"

"It's essential."

"Essential, my ass," Drew barked.

"Give the people what they want," someone in the back yelled.

"For fuck's sake," Drew spat and turned to me. "Why is everyone always trying to get you to take your shirt off?"

"You don't want me to take my shirt off?" I teased, reaching for the buttons to undo one at my chest.

His hand covered mine, stopping the action. "That's a no-brainer, but I would prefer if we were alone."

Leaning in, I whispered, "Think of this as foreplay."

Drew brushed my hand away and undid a button, then another and another, all the way down until the garment was open against my chest.

"It's getting hot in here!" David whistled. "Music!"

Music started playing, and Drew's knuckles brushed over the center of my stomach, making my muscles ripple.

"Now the rest of the shirt," David hollered.

"That guy is a pervert." Drew decided. "I don't like it, T."

"I'm yours, Drew. No one else's."

He hummed, fingers gliding up my chest once more.

"Say it again."

"I'm yours."

He moved closer, our lower bodies colliding, and my hand slid over his hip. Drew's fingers slipped beneath my shirt, pushing it off my shoulder and revealing my chest.

"Fan!" someone yelled.

The sound of a fan clicked on, and a gust of air blew in from the side, picking up the end of my shirt and blowing it away from my body. The scarf around Drew's neck blew forward, concealing part of his face. I tugged it from his body and let go, allowing the manmade wind to carry it away.

Our eyes collided, and I lost myself in him. In the way we were together. His palm settled on my chest, right above the heart that beat just for him.

"Everything in this world seems to have a limit," I whispered. "Except my love for you."

His arms wound around my neck, and our lips met, kissing right there under the sun with an audience we forgot existed.

"It's giving couple goals," someone said around the flash of the camera.

"Definite best-seller energy."

"Okay! Cut! My muse has been satisfied!"

"That's a wrap!"

But we kept kissing.

GEARSHARK PRESENTS

TRENT & DREW MASK
AN EXCLUSIVE INTERVIEW BY EMILY METCALF

Interview key:

GS = *GearShark* (that's me, Emily!)
DM = Drew Mask
TM = Trent Mask

GS: *Can you believe it's been over a decade since I first sat down with you for an interview?*

DM: *Frankly, Emily, I'm shocked you still work here.*

GS: *And why is that?*

<I know by the smile on his face that he's about to say something ornery.>

DM: *Honestly? I thought you'd have bagged a driver by now and ridden off into the sunset.*

GS: <holds up left hand to flash my ring> *Who said I didn't bag myself a driver?*

TM: *It was only a matter of time. Congratulations, Em. Can I call you Em?*

GS: *As long as I don't call you mine, right, Drew?*

DM: *You could try. But then this interview would be over before it got started.*

GS: <laughs> *Still as possessive as ever. I heard you grumbling over the photoshoot earlier.*

DM: <scowls> *All your photographers are pervs, Emily.*

<Trent glances at Drew and smiles.>

TM: *Saltier than a fresh bag of fries. Um, didn't Emily try to hit on you during your first interview?*

<In my defense, wouldn't you?>

GS: *What can I say? I have a thing for adrenaline junkies. Besides, I never stood a chance against you, Trent.*

DM: *Well, that's true. But I'm glad you found your happily-ever-after, Em. I bet you keep your husband on his toes.*

GS: *Thank you, and of course I do. But this interview isn't about me. It's about you.*

DM: *Nosy as ever.*

GS: *Yes, and I've managed to make it into a paying career.*

<Trent laughs and draws the eye of every person within earshot.>

GS: *I think I'll start with something everyone in the room is wondering. How is it you've managed to look even better with age, Trent? What is your anti-aging secret?*

TM: *I don't have any anti-aging secrets because I'm all for aging. I want all the time I can get with my family. Maybe I look good because I'm happy.* <looks at the man beside him> *Because I get to live life with Drew.*

DM: *Not even five minutes in and you're making me blush, frat boy.*

TM: *I like it when you blush.*

GS: *I should have known you wouldn't just recommend a moisturizer.*

TM: <laughs> *I'll have my sister send over a list of skin care recommendations. I just use what she tells me to use.*

DM: *Moisturizer won't make you look like Trent. His beauty isn't skin-deep.*

TM: *I'm not beautiful.*

GS: *Should we take a poll? Let our readers weigh in?*

TM: *Please, no.*

DM: *Emily, you know better than to suggest a poll telling the world how hot my husband is. Next question.*

GS: *Who does what chore at home?*

TM: *I make Drew's coffee.*

DM: *No one makes coffee like T.*

<Trent reaches over and rests his hand on the back of Drew's neck. Drew leans into the touch.>

DM: *I feed the dog.*

TM: *We usually tag-team the laundry.*

DM: <nods> *I sort and wash. He folds.*

GS: *What about the toilets?*

DM: *Do you really think the world wants to know who cleans our toilets?*

GS: *The world is a strange place. Besides, it's hard to imagine legend Drew Mask with a toilet brush in his hand.*

DM: *Next time, I'll take a selfie, post it online.*

GS: *I bet it would make the news.*

DM: <shakes his head in confusion> *The world really is a strange place.*

TM: *Honestly, we are fortunate that we have a cleaning service that comes to our house and helps us with a lot of the deep cleaning. But in between that, it's whoever gets to it first.*

GS: *Who cooks?*

TM: *Mostly me, but sometimes Drew does. When we first got married, we were both terrible cooks. But having kids made us better.*

DM: <nods> *Our daughter likes to help in the kitchen.*

GS: *Your daughter's name is Andi, right?*

<They smile at each other. It makes me feel like a third wheel.>

DM: *Trent named her after me.*

<These guys are adorable.>

GS: *What does Andi like to cook?*

TM: *She makes cookies with her aunt.*

GS: *Which aunt?*

TM: *Rimmel.*

DM: *And brownies with Ivy.*

GS: *What about at home?*

TM: *Meatballs. She likes rolling them into shape.*

DM: <grins> *And then tries to hug everyone with her gross hands.*

TM: *She's clearly a brat like Drew.*

GS: *Drew is a brat?*

TM: *Just the way I like him.*

GS: *How old is Andi now?*

DM: *Almost twelve.*

GS: *Are you nervous about the teenage years?*

TM: *Nah.*

GS: *No? Most parents dread the terrible teens.*

TM: *I don't dread any years I get with my kids.*

<He genuinely means it.>

GS: *You're a sentimental guy.*

TM: <shrugs>

DM: *He's just a good human.*

GS: *Are you nervous about the teenage years with your daughter, Drew?*

DM: *Nope.*

GS: *Maybe because you've had some practice with your son who just turned seventeen, correct?*

DM: *Yes.*

GS: *What's it like parenting a teenage boy?*

TM: *Parenting isn't always easy. It's hard at times, watching them grow up, because you want to protect them from everything but know you can't. You just have to hope you prepared them well enough.*

DM: *Trent is the best father I know.*

GS: *Even better than you?*

TM: <shakes head adamantly> *No.*

DM: *Yes. Our kids are lucky to have him.*

GS: *As a couple, you've faced a lot of disapproval and hurdles, not just from family but from people you don't even know. How have you dealt with that? Has it caused issues in your relationship?*

DM: *Nothing and no one will ever come between me and Trent.*

GS: *So it's never caused a problem?*

TM: *In the beginning, it was harder. We were young and afraid of what our family and friends would say. I worried it would cost Drew his sponsorship with the NRR. I worried it would make him a target for hate.*

DM: *Trent is a worrywart.*

TM: *I didn't want Drew to be punished for loving me.*

GS to DM*: So you never worried?*

<His blue eyes turn thoughtful for a moment before he slowly nods.>

DM: *Of course I did. I was raised under the weight of expectations. I learned very young to bury who I was and what I wanted in favor of who my parents wanted me to be. Breaking out of that was difficult, and T protected me a lot—more than I realized at the time—and he got hurt for it. I don't like to see my person hurt.*

GS: *You mentioned your parents. Are you still estranged from them, Drew?*

TM: *This isn't something we need to talk about.*

GS: Because it's still painful?

DM: *No. Because we aren't estranged. We aren't anything. They aren't part of my life anymore, so there's no point in discussing them.*

GS: *Point taken. Has it gotten easier to deal with the scrutiny and, to be blunt, the online hate as an out couple in the press and being more of your authentic self?*

TM: *I think hate in any form is hard, and, from my perspective, the more accepting society becomes of queer relationships, the louder the hate gets. The real difference is how we react to it. We used to care what other people thought or what we might lose by being together.*

GS: *And now?*

DM: *Now we don't give a flying fuck. Can I say fuck?*

GS: *You just did. Twice. And in every interview we've ever had.*

TM: *What Drew means is we realized we don't need permission to be who we are. I don't want someone else's hate to take up any space inside me because it would be less that I had for my kids and husband. When I spent a week wondering if I'd already lived all the moments with my most important person and if I'd already said the last words he'd ever hear, it put things in perspective. I thought a lot about the times I didn't kiss him when I wanted to or when I held off on showing him affection when other people were around. Those lost moments were far more fucking painful than someone else's hate.*

DM to TM: *Oooh, you said fuck too.*

TM: <winks at Drew> *Just for you, baby.*

GS: *So it doesn't get easier. You just get better at ignoring it.*

DM: *Oh, we know it's there. We just don't let it define us.*

TM: *We define ourselves.*

GS: *Drew, you mentioned before about growing up with a lot of expectations and feeling unable to be yourself. How has that affected your way of parenting?*

DM: *It taught me how not to be. I want my kids to know they can tell me anything about themselves and their dreams and that I'll support them.*

GS: *Does your son have an interest in cars?*

TM: <laughs> *Calling it an interest would be an understatement.*

DM: *Travis loves cars and driving. We just got him his first car.*

GS: *Make and model?*

<He smiles so wide I can see his dimple beneath the stubble lining his jaw.>

DM: *Guess.*

GS: *I'm going to say a Mustang of some sort.*

TM: *If you had gotten that wrong, Em, I would have questioned your journalistic instincts.*

GS: *Well, Drew is endorsed by Ford. Did they send over a car for him?*

DM & TM in unison: *Hells no.*

DM: *If he wants a car, he has to earn it.*

GS: *So you're making him pay for it?*

TM: *We're making him build it.*

GS: *Build it!*

DM: *Technically, restore it. We found a 1970 Mach 1 that has seen better days, so he's going to have to put in a lot of elbow grease to get it road-ready.*

TM: *A good driver knows what's under his hood and how to handle it.*

GS: *You're helping him restore it?*

DM: *Me and Trent both.*

GS: *Is he a good driver?*

TM: *Trav is good at a lot of things, driving being one of them.*

GS: *You're proud of him.*

TM: *We're proud of both our kids.*

GS: *Has it been hard to shield them from the press?*

DM: *Yes. Some people don't have limits, even with kids.*

GS: *There's been a lot of headlines centering around your kids lately. Especially the birthday party you recently had for your son.*

DM: *You're really going for all the dirt, Emily.*

GS: *I'm asking what the people want to know.*

<Drew looks at Trent.>

TM: *We had a situation not long ago with a woman approaching our daughter, trying to take advantage of her.*

GS: *How?*

<The muscle in Trent's jaw tenses, and his hazel eyes flash with anger.>

TM: *She tried to tell Andi she was her mother.*

GS: *That's a serious allegation. And potentially very harmful to a child.*

DM: *No shit.*

GS: *Do your children know they're adopted?*

TM: *Yes, we've been open about it from the very beginning.*

GS: *Do they ever ask about their birth mother?*

TM: *No.*

GS: *No? Why not?*

DM: *She's dead.*

GS: *Oh. I wasn't aware. I'm sorry to hear about that. Do your children know this as well?*

TM: *Yes, they've always known. It's just something we haven't spoken about in the press because our children have the right to privacy. Just because we're in the spotlight doesn't mean they have to be.*

GS: *These recent headlines must be upsetting for you.*

DM: *Of course they are. People are getting bold—too bold—and approaching them. It shouldn't have to be said, but I'd like to remind the press and general public that our children are off-limits.*

GS: *Can you tell us what happened? From the perspective of a parent, not a headline.*

TM: *We'd been getting letters for three months from a woman claiming to be our children's birth mother, which we ignored in an attempt to not escalate the situation. We had no reason to believe she would approach our kids.*

GS: *But she did.*

TM: *Yes. She approached both Travis and Andi at an ice cream shop.*

GS: *What was your daughter's reaction to this stranger approaching her?*

DM: *She was confused. And afraid.*

GS: *A few headlines claim that your son got physical with the woman.*

DM: *What did you expect him to do? Allow his sister to be kidnapped?*

GS: *So she did try and kidnap her?*

TM: *Yes. She tried to make Andi get into her car.*

GS: *But your son stopped her, and the woman ran off?*

DM: *Yes, she left before the police got to the scene.*

GS: *Romeo Anderson's daughter was also there, wasn't she?*

DM: *Yes, she was.*

GS: None of the children were hurt?

TM: *No. Our son, Travis, removed the girls from the situation.*

GS: *Recently, this woman gained access to your family compound that you share with Romeo Anderson, Braeden Walker, and their families. Specifically, during your son's birthday party.*

TM: *Yes.*

GS: *Isn't your family property very secure? How did she gain access?*

DM: *She snuck into a vehicle that was being delivered.*

GS: *A vehicle? Wasn't anyone driving it? Didn't they notice?*

TM: *It was on a flatbed truck. It was a birthday gift for our son.*

GS: *The Mach 1 you got him?*

DM: *No. This was another car.*

GS: *Someone else bought your son a car for his birthday? Who?*

<They had to know I'd ask. I mean, we all want to know!>

DM: *It was from Ron Gamble.*

GS: *Ron Gamble, owner of the NRR and Maryland Knights, bought your son a car?*

TM: *He only owns part of the NRR. But to our son, he's just Grampy.*

DM: *Oooh, frat boy. You did it now. Just wait 'til this is printed.*

<Trent laughs.>

GS: *Care to pour me some of that tea, boys?*

DM: *Let me just say, you should never refer to Ron Gamble as Grampy.*

GS: *Noted. So back to the stowaway inside your son's birthday gift that was NOT from Grampy.* <Snickering ensues.> *What happened?*

DM: <all traces of humor gone now> *She waited until our daughter was alone and attacked, tying her hands and covering her mouth so she couldn't yell or get away.*

TM: *And then she attempted to leave the property with our daughter, using one of our four-wheelers.*

GS: *Oh my gosh, this sounds scary. How did you stop her?*

DM: *Trent knocked the woman off the quad and basically sat on her until the police arrived.*

GS: *And where is this woman now?*

TM: *In custody. Getting the help she needs.*

GS: *For the record, there is absolutely no chance she could be your children's birth mother?*

TM: *No chance in hell.*

GS: *How are your children now after everything?*

TM: *They're doing fine. We all want to move on.*

<I think that's my not-so-subtle cue to change the subject.>

GS: *Your self-proclaimed brother, Romeo Anderson, retired last year after a glistening fifteen-year career with the Maryland Knights. How has he been enjoying retired life?*

DM: <laughs> *Considering he's already at Alpha University as their new head coach, I'd say he's not really retired.*

TM: *Football is in Rome's blood. He'll always be doing it in one way or another, but it is nice to have him closer to home.*

GS: *Speaking of retirement...*

DM: ...

TM: ...

GS: *You're going to make me ask?*

DM: *Ask what?*

GS: *Good thing you're a better driver than actor.*

TM: *I don't know. I bet he'd do well on the big screen. Look at those eyes.*

DM: *I've been on TV.*

GS: *Yes, but you play yourself.*

<I'm referring to his sponsorship and endorsement deals.>

DM: *Have you been listening to rumors, Emily?*

GS: *So the headlines claiming you are retiring from driving are rumors?*

<Drew and Trent share a look. Trent smiles patiently and links their hands.>

DM: *Maybe not just a rumor.*

GS: *You're confirming that you plan to retire from the NRR?*

DM: *When I came back after my accident twelve years ago, I hadn't planned on racing this long. I'd only come back because I didn't want to go out like that. I intended to drive a few more seasons and then hang up my helmet.*

GS: *And here we are twelve years later.*

TM: *Driving is in his DNA.*

DM to TM: *So are you.*

GS: *So why now?*

DM: *I want to spend more time at home with my kids. With Trent. I'm proud of what I've achieved. Plus, I'm not getting any younger.*

GS: *So you're tired?*

DM: *Not so much tired as ready to move on.*

GS: *To what?*

DM: *I'm still working that out.*

GS: *Do you plan to leave motorsports altogether, or will you stay in some capacity, like as a broadcaster or maybe as a performance coach? Your brothers, Braeden and Romeo, both took on coaching jobs after retirement.*

DM: *I'm still working that out.*

GS: *That's all you're going to give me, huh?*

TM: *I think he's earned some time off.*

<I tried, guys, tried to find out all the details, but these boys stayed mum.>

GS: *It's really hard to imagine racing without Drew Mask.*

DM: *I'll be around.*

<Could he be any more mysterious?>

GS: *So for the record, you are verifying that you, Drew Mask, plan to retire from racing in the NRR?*

DM: *This is me verifying my plans to retire.*

GS: *Have you discussed this with your on-track rival and off-track friend Jace Lorhaven?*

TM: *He's even nosier than you, Emily.*

DM: <laughs> *I've talked to him, yes.*

GS: *And what does he think about your plans?*

DM: *He's supportive.*

GS: *Wow, don't overload me with details, guys.*

DM: *You could always call and ask him yourself.*

GS: *I just might.*

GS: *You just talked about how you never intended to drive for as long as you have after your comeback from the on-track crash that nearly claimed your life—*

TM: *I'd rather talk about Lorhaven. I can give you some gossip.*

GS: *Well, my interest is piqued.*

TM: *He's been banned from at least two bars for excessive use of jazz hands.*

<Drew throws back his head and laughs.>

GS: <skeptical> *Lorhaven, the bad boy of the NRR, uses jazz hands?*

TM: *I saw his journal once. He says he isn't a bad boy but a misunderstood villain.*

GS: *His diary...*

DM: *Stop causing trouble, frat boy. Thanksgiving is going to be a shit show.*

GS: *You spend Thanksgiving with Lorhaven?*

DM: *He's family.*

GS to TM: *You still don't like talking about his accident, do you?*

TM: *Obviously.*

GS: *Even after all this time?*

TM: *Always.*

GS: *My question isn't really about the accident, more about what came after.*

<Drew gestures for me to ask.>

GS: *How hard was it getting back to normal after the accident?*

DM: *We didn't go back to normal because our normal changed.*

TM: <nods> *It got better.*

GS: *Because you became parents?*

DM: *Because we were still together. Because the accident was terrible, but it gave us the courage to live full throttle. I don't think I really realized how much I held back until I almost died.*

GS: *I never thought of you as a man who holds back.*

DM: *On the track, definitely not. But in other aspects of life, in relationships, it was harder to come out of my shell.*

GS: *What does coming out of your shell mean exactly?*

DM: *Being vulnerable.*

GS: *But now you are?*

<Drew glances at Trent, and they share a look I can only describe as intimate and *hot.*>

DM: *Yeah.*

GS: *How hard was it getting back on the track and behind the wheel?*

DM: *It was hard. The hardest thing I've ever done in my career.*

GS: *What was that first time behind the wheel of your race car like?*

DM: *I had a panic attack.*

GS: *Really?*

<Drew hums, and he and Trent start having a conversation with their eyes.>

GS: *What are you saying to each other?*

TM: *Not really saying anything. Just remembering.*

DM: *Trent got in the car with me. Sat in the driver's seat and pulled me into his lap.*

GS: *Was there enough room for that?*

TM: <laughs> *No. But we made it work.*

DM: *T drove partway around the track at a turtle's pace with me sitting in his lap, sweating through my suit and shaking like a leaf.*

TM: *You put your hands over mine on the steering wheel and helped steer.*

<I'm pretty sure if I got out a tape measure to calculate the chemistry nearly suffocating this room, I'd run out of tape before I could measure it all.>

GS: *Did it help?*

DM: <flashes a bright smile> *I'm sitting here, aren't I?*

GS: *Trent, how hard was that day for you? And watching him race again?*

TM: *I didn't think about me that day. I concentrated on him and doing everything I could to help him in that moment and then after to get back to his dream.*

GS: *You aren't scared when he drives?*

TM: *I'm not scared of Drew driving because he's the best driver*

I know. But, of course, I worry about him. We all worry about the people we love.

GS: *Drew, how long would you say it took to be comfortable driving again?*

DM: *Six months. Sometimes I still have intrusive flashbacks.*

GS: *Really?*

DM: *Occasionally. My PTSD is well-managed, but every once in a while, something triggers it. But I'm not controlled by it anymore.*

<Trent puts his hand on the back of Drew's neck again, and Drew visibly relaxes.>

TM: *It's not a sign of weakness. Trauma changes the brain. He's worked hard to get to where he is, and I'm proud of him.*

GS to TM: *I think maybe you've helped him a lot too.*

DM: *He's the reason I'm here today.*

TM to DM: *You're strong all on your own, baby.*

DM to TM: *But I'm stronger with you.*

<Sitting here with them makes me feel very single… and I'm married. Let's hope my hubby doesn't read this!>

GS: *Drew, who has the best French fries?*

DM: *Ooooooh, you had to go there.*

GS: *I think it's only fair that such a known fry connoisseur shares his knowledge with the people. We all want good fries.*

DM: *I like all fries.*

GS: *Okay, but what is your favorite?*

DM: *The thick-cut ones, no fancy seasoning. Freshly fried in peanut oil and then salted while they're still hot. Serve them with a side of ketchup—Heinz only—and that is my favorite plate of fries.*

GS: *Doesn't that ketchup brand sponsor you?*

DM: *Yes, but I would say the same thing with or without the sponsorship. They are the only ketchup.*

TM: *It's true.*

GS: *What have you learned during your career as a professional driver?*

DM: *That I love speed, but sometimes it's good to slow down.*

GS: *What do you consider your greatest accomplishment so far?*

DM: *Trent and my kids.*

GS: *More specifically, in racing?*

DM: *Having the guts to reach for my dreams. All my trophies are pretty cool too.*

GS to TM: *We've talked a lot about Drew and his career, but nothing about yours.*

TM: *This is* GearShark, *a racing magazine. I don't drive.*

GS: *That one time, you did. With Drew in your lap.*

TM: *I'd do anything for Drew.*

GS: You do work with the NRR in a prominent position given to you by Ron Gamble himself.

DM: *Trent earned his job. He's a genius in business.*

GS: *I have no doubt about that. You also serve as Drew's spotter at all his races, right?*

TM: *Yes.*

GS: *How do you both balance such demanding careers while raising two kids?*

TM: *I have a lot of flexibility with my job. I can do it from home or on the road with Drew. Plus, we have an amazing family that helps when we need them.*

GS: *Where do you see yourselves in five years?*

TM: *Together and happy.*

DM: *What he said.*

GS: *Nothing more specific?*

TM: *Nothing else matters.*

GS: *Are you up for a few rapid-fire questions before we end the interview?*

DM: *Bring it.*

GS: *One word to describe your partner in the morning.*

<Trent belts out a laugh, and Drew rolls his eyes.>

TM: *Cranky.*

DM: *Too happy.*

GS: *That's two words, Drew.*

DM: *Sue me.*

GS: *Who said I love you first?*

DM: *Trent.*

GS: *If you had to be handcuffed together for twenty-four hours, what would go wrong first?*

TM: <smirks> *Nothing. I'd like it.*

GS: *What is your favorite thing the other wears?*

DM: *I like when he wears my boxers.*

TM: *His wedding ring.*

GS: *Favorite holiday?*

TM & DM: *Christmas.*

GS: *Who gets hangry first?*

TM: *Drew.*

GS: *Who's the better kisser?*

TM: *Drew.*

DM: *Trent.*

GS: *You two have been good sports today, and you've answered a lot of tough questions. On behalf of* GearShark, *thank you for sitting down with us. And personally, it's been great to see you both again. You truly are one of my favorites to interview.*

TM: *It was great seeing you again, Em.*

And that, devoted *GearShark* readers, is in the in-depth gab sesh that I had with these true icons, Trent and Drew Mask.

Drew might be driving toward retirement, but the mark he left on the racing world and in all our hearts is forever permanent. And honestly, he might be hanging up his racing suit, but this journalist has a feeling we haven't seen the last of either of these men.

You can rest assured that we here at *GearShark* will keep

our eyes peeled for whatever these boys get up to next. And who knows? Maybe someday their son will be gracing our pages and burning up the track with all that adrenaline he inherited.

15

Drew

The chiming of my phone was such a cockblock.

I tried to ignore it, but the fourth time it chirped, I pulled off of Trent's cock and let out an exasperated huff. "Seriously."

Above me, Trent laughed, and I shoved the blankets back and sat up between his naked thighs. "If we didn't have kids, I'd flush those fuckers right now."

His eyes strayed down to the boner tenting my boxer briefs and lingered.

"*Frat boy*," I whined, which was completely uncalled for, but I wanted my mouth back on him.

Trent chuckled, the throaty sound only making it worse, and flung out his hand to grab a phone and check the screen.

His loud laugh burst through the room, making me scowl. "What?"

"The *GearShark* article released," Trent said, still staring at his phone.

"That was today?"

"Guess so," he said. "Everyone's sending photos of it out in the wild."

"Who cares?" I said, eyes straying back to his dick. It was still hard, the tip shiny from my mouth, and—

"Lorhaven is pissed."

I burst out laughing.

"Says he's going to use his jazz hands and slap us into next week."

"He'd have to catch me first," I mused, settling back between his thighs and wrapping my fist around his girth.

He grunted, and I gave it a squeeze, pushing it up against his stomach to suck one of his balls into my mouth and tug.

His knees bent a little, so I sucked harder, making his feet draw up until they were flat on the mattress. A hot wave of lust shot through me, and I thrust against the mattress. Still gripping his cock, I released his sack to push my face between his cheeks.

Trent arched a little, making a sound before widening his legs to give me more room. Groaning, I settled in, lavishing his hole with my tongue.

"The cover turned out pretty good," he said, his voice a little out of it.

I grunted in reply and kept licking while working his dick.

"They went with the one of me with my shirt open."

I froze mid lick.

"You wanna see?"

I lifted my head just enough to look up the long length of his torso. Trent tilted the screen down so I could see the photo filling it.

And there we were.

Me in my track suit and him looking like a fucking thirst

trap. But what was even better was the way that thirst trap was looking at me. Like I was all he saw.

I'm yours.

I grabbed the phone out of his hand and tossed it over the bed before diving between his legs, spearing him with my tongue.

He cursed, and I did it again. "*Mine.*"

He tried to laugh, but it turned into a drawn-out moan as I put my fingers where my tongue had been.

"I'm not sharing you."

"I don't want you to."

I kissed my way up his dick and chest until I was over him. "I want you, T. I want you so bad."

"You have me. Anytime you want."

It had been a while since I topped Trent. Usually, I wanted him on me, over me. Everywhere. But just then, I felt the need to claim him even if he already was mine.

I lowered onto him, pressing us together from legs to lips. His weight easily accepted mine, and though his body was hard, Trent was always a soft place for me to fall. The kiss was deep and thorough, me inventorying everything about him that I already knew. I'd been here a thousand times and likely would a thousand more, but no two times with Trent were ever quite the same.

Licking into his mouth, I shoved my hand under the pillow, feeling around for the hidden bottle of lube. I pulled back, ripping our lips apart to kiss across his jaw and into his neck. We moved together like an ocean wave, ebbing and flowing but our bodies in sync.

Our cocks slotted together between our bodies was the perfect friction, building the need inside me until I could think of nothing else.

Sliding down his body, I mouthed at him as I went, kissing, sucking, and nipping at every part of him I could touch as I settled on my knees between his thighs.

His cock jerked to the sound of the cap popping open, and I leaned over to slide him into the back of my throat. His moan was guttural and deep, the throbbing of his cock a rhythm against my tongue.

Leaving my lips around him, I poured some lube onto my fingertips and massaged it around his entrance, swirling my fingers in a circle until his hips were moving to the same tempo. His breath caught when my finger breached him, and I pulled off his cock to sit up and watch the pleasure play over his face.

I loved him like this. My big, strong husband reduced to a shivering pile of want with flushed cheeks, hazy eyes, and kiss-reddened lips. His chest rose and fell heavily with his panting, and his hair was mussed from the way his head thrashed on the pillow.

When he was ready, I worked a second finger into him, both of us groaning at the way his body just sucked me right in.

"You are so hot like this, T," I whispered, adding more lube to his ass and scissoring my fingers open.

Impatience created a second heartbeat inside me, demanding I get inside him faster.

"More, baby," he murmured, pushing back on my fingers.

I curled them in, brushing over that textured spot inside him, and he let out a guttural sound. "That's my spot," I told him, sliding in a third finger. "That's a place only I know how to find, only I know how to pleasure."

"Only you," he echoed, abs contracting.

I gave it another stroke, enjoying the way his body sang, before pulling out and pushing down my boxers to slick up my desperate cock.

He watched me stroke myself through half-slitted lids, gnawing on his lower lip like he wanted to beg.

"I love you like this," I confessed. "My dominant husband on his back for me, legs spread, with a look of desperation glinting in your eyes."

"I want you, Drew. Come over here and give it to me."

My hands hit the mattress on either side of his body, and his hands curled around my forearms. I rocked against his prepped hole, reveling at the softness of his ring versus the granite of my head. "You ready?"

"Take me, Drew."

I shoved in, claiming my rightful place inside him with a single stroke. Both of us groaned in bliss, and I dropped my head between my shoulders as a full-body shiver ran down to my toes. He was hot and tight, the grip on me possessive and unrelenting.

I pulled back and snapped my hips, forcing a grunt out of him that curled my toes. I started thrusting then, hammering into his body as though it were my life's mission, all my attention condensed to the place our bodies intersected.

"Mine," I growled, thrusting again and again. "Mine. Mine. Mine."

Trent's hips lifted off the bed, and I reached around to fill my palm with his ass. Between us, his dick bounced, slapping against his stomach, smearing everything it touched.

When he collapsed against the mattress, I fisted his cock and started jacking him to the tune of my thrusts.

"Drew." He panted, body straining.

"Come on, frat boy," I said, still working him inside and out. "Squeeze my dick with how hard you come."

One final thrust and I hit his swollen prostate, making his mouth open, but no sound came out. His body went stiff as his cock erupted, shooting ropes of white cum out across his chest and stomach. His ass clenched so hard it triggered my orgasm, and I threw my head back and moaned into the ceiling as wave after wave of ecstasy rolled over me. My eyes were open, but I stopped seeing, held prisoner by the intensity of the release.

When it finally let go, I collapsed on top of him, and he wrapped his thick thighs around me, anchoring me against him. I was still buried inside him, and he squeezed his arms around me tight.

"I fucking needed that," I murmured after a while, languid as hell.

His chest shook with silent laughter, and he kissed the side of my head. "Me too, baby."

I snuggled a little closer, loving the sound of his after-sex voice.

Oh, who am I kidding? I loved the sound of his voice always.

"Let me see that magazine cover again," I said, making no move to get off him.

"You threw my phone on the floor."

I leaned over and grabbed my phone, flopping back into his chest.

He took it and unlocked it. "Here," he said, holding up the photo.

I looked up, studying the colorful image for a few moments and then dismissing it to bury my face in his neck.

"Well?" he asked.

"You're too hot."

His laugh was loud around the bedroom. "Me? Did you see how you looked in that suit with all that blond hair?"

"As if anyone will notice with you standing there like Fabio with your shirt blowing in the wind."

"Are you jealous?" he asked.

"No. I'm territorial."

"Well, I'd say you just marked your territory."

"Hmm, I did." I agreed, feeling very proud of myself.

"I love this life," he whispered, the words hitting me straight in my feels. "It's better than I could ever have imagined."

Every hardship we'd ever been through seemed like small potatoes compared to his happiness. Like the really small potatoes, ones not even suitable for fries.

"I love it too, T," I whispered back. "Even more than French fries."

The End

Not really. Turn the page for a Bonus Scene!

BONUS SCENE

BECAUSE WHAT ABOUT NOVA'S DATE!?

Trent

Drew and I walked through the sliders and into the kitchen to find Braeden and Romeo at the island.

Based on the sour and sulking expression on B's face, no wonder Romeo texted.

"What's going on?" I asked, looking between the pair.

Romeo didn't look quite as perturbed as B, but he wasn't exactly carefree either.

"I'll tell you what's going on," Braeden grumped. "That kid hasn't had enough brain injuries on the field. His memory still works too well."

I glanced at Drew, and we shared a look.

Romeo grunted. "If you were him, would you forget a date with the most popular girl at school?"

"That kid is still sniffing around Nova?" Drew asked, going to the fridge for a soda. "Maybe his brain is damaged if he's still dogging at her heels for a date even after that debacle at Travis's birthday party."

"No one said he was smart," Braeden remarked.

"There's not smart, and then there's just stupid." Drew went on. "Someone came onto the property, tried to kidnap one of us, and then Trent charged a four-wheeler to take her down. He physically sat on her until the cops came."

"He's thinking with his dick," Romeo declared, and we all nodded.

Dude was definitely thinking with his dick.

Braeden lurched up from the stool. "I'll kill him."

"I know you four aren't in here having some kind of man meeting about Nova going to the movies tonight," Ivy said, walking into the kitchen with a pair of UGG slippers on her feet.

Shaking her blond head, she continued to the kettle to put some water on to boil.

"How can you be so calm about this, blondie?"

"Because it's the movies, not some rave. You can't expect a beautiful girl like her to just sit at home forever."

"This is what I get for marrying a bombshell. Should have found someone without a face card," Braeden mourned.

We all laughed.

Except for Ivy.

Rimmel strolled in, dark hair in two braids and her usual oversized sweats hanging on her hips. "What's going on in here?" She glanced around. "Oh geez, are you having a man meeting about Nova's date?"

"Yeah, so no girls allowed," Braeden retorted.

Rimmel ignored him and went to the cupboard. "We're making apple cider." She stretched up on her tiptoes for a mug, fingers still not reaching. With a sound, she lowered and was about to climb on the counter when Romeo stepped in.

"Hold your horses there, smalls. We don't have time for

an ER visit tonight," he told her, grabbing her around the waist and lifting her off her feet.

Rim looked over her shoulder at him and smiled. "It would be a good distraction for Nova."

"I won't have it," he said, holding her with one arm and reaching into the cabinet for two mugs.

"Thank you," she said sweetly.

He made a gruff sound. "Make your cider and stay out of trouble."

"Us!" Ivy declared. "You four are the ones in here talking about brain injury and murder!"

Rimmel gasped. "What?"

"Were you listening at the door?" Drew asked.

"This is my house." Ivy sniffed and then turned to B. "I'm telling you right now, Braeden. You let our daughter have her first date. Do not try and intimidate that boy when he comes to pick her up."

"This is my house," he said, using her words against her.

The kettle started whistling, but Ivy ignored it to stroll forward with a spoon in her hand. "Braeden James, do not interfere with her date," Ivy warned, poking him in the center of his chest with the spoon.

Rimmel came over with a spoon of her own and poked him too. "Or. Else."

"You better get your girl, Rome."

Both girls turned to Romeo, brandishing the spoons.

He laughed.

They went about making mugs of steaming cider, and Rimmel opened another cabinet before turning to bat her eyes at Romeo.

He shook his head and reached in, pulling out a jar of cinnamon sticks. When she moved to take them, he held them just out of reach. Rimmel rolled her eyes but then pursed her lips. Only after she kissed him did he hand over the jar.

"Mom! I have nothing to wear!" Nova yelled down the stairs like it was an actual national emergency.

"Now, I know that's a lie," Braeden quipped. "That girl has more clothes than some small countries."

"Aunt Rimmel!"

"She must really be desperate if she's asking for Rimmel's help with an outfit," I teased.

Rimmel planted her hands on her hips and glared at me. "I've learned a lot from Ivy over the years."

"Yet you're still standing there in Rome's old sweats," Drew teased.

"And whose shirt are you wearing right now, Drew?" Rimmel asked.

I glanced at what he was wearing—a shirt she'd bought me for Christmas last year—and laughed.

"*Mom!*"

"We're coming!" Ivy hollered to Nova. Then to Rimmel, "We'd better get up there before she does something drastic."

"Like pick her own outfit?" Romeo wondered.

"Maybe she'll cancel her date." Braeden hoped.

"This is our punishment for having kids with them," Ivy lamented.

Rimmel nodded emphatically.

"We're going upstairs. When he comes to the door, let him inside. Do *not* pretend we aren't home," Ivy told us.

"Do not intimidate him either."

"Are we intimidating, or is he just intimidated?" Romeo wondered.

"Neither. He's horny." Drew decided.

Ivy and Rimmel both turned to stare at us over their still-steaming mugs. It made them both look kinda creepy.

"This includes both of you. We're watching," Ivy intoned.

Rimmel pointed to her eyes and then at us with two fingers. It wasn't scary. Her hands were the size of Andi's.

"Yes, ma'am," Drew and I replied in unison, and the girls left.

When they were gone, the four of us looked at each other for a long, silent minute.

"So we're following them, right?" Braeden finally decided.

"Of course." Drew agreed.

"I'll drive," Romeo added.

I had to contribute something. "We'll wear hats."

Everyone nodded.

About fifteen minutes later, the doorbell rang. All the dogs barked and raced into the entryway. Braeden wound through all the chaos and wrapped his hand around the door handle.

"Sick him!" B told the dogs and then opened the door.

Night air spilled in from the front porch, met with a gaggle of barking dogs. Jordan jumped back a step at the burst of anarchy as dogs swarmed around him, yapping and sniffing the newcomer.

"Oh, my bad, Falls," Braeden said. "These dogs are just hard to control."

"It's okay, Coach Walker," Jordan said, holding his hand out to Rocket. "Hey, Rocket, remember me from practices?"

Rocket stopped barking and licked his hand.

"Traitor," Braeden hissed.

The wind blew a few leaves across the driveway, and the dogs went bounding into the yard after them.

"That your car?" Drew asked.

Jordan turned to glance at the Nissan parked nearby. "Yes, sir."

"You should have bought a Ford," Drew replied, going down the steps to open the passenger door and look inside. "You got a full tank of gas?"

"Y-yeah...?"

"You don't sound sure. A good driver always knows how much gas he has in his tank."

"It's like three-quarters," Jordan said.

"And the theater is, what, twenty minutes away?" I surmised. "That means you have plenty to get there and back. We don't want to hear the *I ran out of gas* line."

"Okay." Jordan agreed.

Braeden crossed his arms over his chest. "I want her home by eleven."

"Eleven-oh-two is late," Romeo told him.

"Yes, sir," Jordan agreed.

Uncrossing his arms, Braeden stepped closer to Jordan. "I'm not your coach tonight, Falls. Tonight, I'm the father of a girl you're taking out. You know what that means?"

"Uh, no..."

"It means you will keep your hands above the waist all night, your dick stays in your pants, and that tongue stays in your mouth. You got me?"

"Y-yes, sir."

"Dad!" Nova said, appearing through the open front door. "What did you say to him?"

"Nothing. We were just talking football," Braeden said, plastering on a smile. "Right, Jordan?"

"Yeah, football." He agreed, then turned his full attention to her.

My niece was dressed in a pair of light-wash jeans and a tight camel-colored top with a square neckline. Her long dark hair was down around her shoulders and curled in loose waves. In her hand was a cream-colored bag with an oversized braided texture.

"You look great," Jordan told her. "Really pretty."

"Really?" Nova asked, batting her eyes at him.

Ah, young love.

He nodded.

"Thanks. I love your jacket." She complimented his varsity jacket.

Braeden made a sound, and Ivy elbowed him.

"You two have a good time," Ivy said, shooing us all into the house. "What movie are you going to see?"

"*Clara,*" Nova answered. "You know, the new one about that AI doll that like goes crazy and kills everyone."

"A horror movie!" Braeden roared from inside the house. "Oh, hells no!"

"Come on. Let's go." Nova pulled Jordan off the porch and toward his Nissan.

"Eleven o'clock!" Braeden reminded, reappearing on the porch.

"*Braeden,*" Ivy hissed.

"You'd better open that door for her," I called.

"Trent, get in the house," Rimmel demanded from the doorway.

Braeden and I were the last inside. The second the door shut, Braeden erupted.

"A horror movie, Blondie," Braeden exclaimed. "That little shit."

"What's wrong with a horror movie?" Rimmel asked.

Braeden made a rude sound. "The only reason a guy takes a girl to a scary movie is so she'll get scared and cling to him."

"It's true," I echoed.

"So they hold hands, or he puts his arm around her," Ivy said. "Let her have fun tonight."

"How about we have a movie night of our own?" Rimmel suggested. "It will help pass the time until Nova gets home and can tell us about her date."

"Ooh, love that." Ivy agreed.

"That's a good idea," Romeo said, and B whipped around

to glare at him like he'd lost his mind. But he kept talking. "I'll go grab some pizza at the shop we like in town."

"We can just order it," Ivy said.

"No point in making them drive all the way out here to the compound. It just interrupts their delivery schedule," he said, and Braeden nodded.

"We'll give them a big tip," Rimmel reasoned.

"It's Friday night. They're probably busy," Braeden refuted. "I'll go too."

"Why do you need to go?" Ivy asked, suspicious.

"Because it's a lot of pizza. He needs help."

"You know what goes good with pizza? Ice cream," Drew said.

I nodded. "We'll come too. Get the dessert."

"Wait a minute." Ivy started, but all four of us were already up and moving to the door.

"You pick a movie, baby. We'll be back with the food," Romeo said, kissing Rimmel on the head on his way out the door.

"We'll be right back!" Braeden called, diving into the back of Romeo's SUV. (The Hellcat was parked inside the garage.)

"Drive!" Drew said.

Romeo took off down the road. "Think they were on to us?"

"Definitely," I mused.

"Keep driving, Rome," Braeden ordered.

Twenty-five minutes later, we had tickets in hand and were walking into theater number eight. The large space was dark and cool, and the previews had already started.

We stood off to the side, against the wall in the shadows, peering through the rows of people in search of Nova and her date.

"Where the hell are they?" Braeden muttered. "I swear, if

he didn't bring her where he said, I will feed his balls to the dogs."

"There," Drew said, gesturing with his chin. "In the middle row."

"They got good seats," I remarked.

"Right?" Drew replied.

"Focus," Braeden demanded.

"Go up that way and around the top," Romeo directed. "Then come down to that empty row a few up from them."

"You see his hands?" Braeden asked, staring hard.

"They're eating popcorn," I said, watching him shovel it in.

"There's only one drink," Romeo observed.

"Ew, are they sharing?" Braeden panicked. "No telling where that kid's mouth has been."

"Let's go," Drew whispered, and we made our way to the row Romeo chose and sank into the chairs about four rows behind Nova and Jordan.

Another preview came on, one about some kind of creature under someone's bed, and frankly, it was unsettling. Seconds later, Drew jolted when the creature shot out from the darkness.

"*Shit*," he swore beneath his breath.

I draped my arm around him, pulling him close. "I'll protect you, baby."

"See, that right there," B said, pointing at us accusingly.

We turned toward the kids just as Jordan put his arm around Nova who was covering her eyes. She leaned in, and the little shit went as far as pushing up the armrest between them so he could move closer.

Braeden leaned over to the couple next to him. "You mind?"

Before they could reply, he grabbed a fistful of their

popcorn and tossed it a few rows down so it hit Jordan in the head.

The kids pulled apart to look behind them, and Braeden dropped into his chair.

The four of us did our best to shrink into the seats, but Nova was like her mother. "You have got to be kidding," she exclaimed.

People turned to look.

Another preview started playing.

"You made the movie sound good, Critter. We decided to come watch too," Braeden hollered.

"*Shhh*!" the people behind us hissed.

Jordan and Nova turned back in their seats and sank down, heads together.

About five minutes later, Jordan slid his arm around Nova again. All four of us coughed, and he pulled it back.

Nova turned to glare over the seats but turned back as the movie started to play.

"Hey, this looks pretty good," Drew murmured, pushing the armrest up to lean farther into my side. I laughed under my breath.

We made it ten more minutes before movement at the end of the aisle had me turning my head.

I jolted, and Drew laughed. "It got you too," he said.

Grabbing his chin, I pulled his face around.

"*Oh shit*," he swore.

"Hey," I called to Romeo and B.

They turned, eyes seeing the same thing Drew just had.

Ivy and Rimmel stood at the end of the row. Hands on hips. Glaring fiercely.

"Ah, baby, what are you doing here?" Braeden asked.

"Really, Braeden?" she intoned.

"I thought you were getting pizza," Rimmel deadpanned.

"Well…"

Both of them shook their heads and pointed.

Someone onscreen let out a blood-curdling scream.

The four of us exchanged looks and then filed out of the row.

"I cannot believe you," Ivy chastised.

"You've gone too far," Rimmel lectured.

I looked over at Nova and her date as we passed. They waved.

"I hope they enjoy the rest of their night," Drew murmured. "Because we sure as hell won't."

AUTHOR'S NOTE

When I looked at the calendar and realized *#Junkie* was turning ten, I was frankly, flabbergasted. I mean, how the heck did the last ten years go by so fast? And then I realized that Trent & Drew have spent the last decade at the very top of my favorite list. Frankly, I find that impressive. I have a lot of books. A lot of characters that have stolen my heart. A few couples have come close to the pedestal #trew are perched on. But they have yet to be dethroned. These two… these two just have something special. I've thought about it over the years, wondering what it is that they have that just makes them so unbeatable (to me). There are a lot of reasons, but I always come back to *something* I can't quite name. They just really make me *feel.*

And not to be dramatic, but this book, this couple, changed my life. They altered the way I write and the way I think. They truly left a mark (on me) that is still here after a decade. *#Junkie* was my first male/male romance novel. My first gay couple. I learned so much about love and acceptance from them. I learned the beauty of diversity. They helped me grow not only as a writer but as a person. Because of them,

I've gone on to write many more MM romance novels. I've also tried to add more diversity into my work in other ways (disabilities, ethnicity, socioeconomic backgrounds).

So of course I had to do something for their anniversary. They deserve it.

As I've said in the past, coming back to any *Hashtag* and *GearShark* book is always a little intimidating for me. It's silly that my own characters have the ability to intimidate me, but to me, they've just sort of become this big thing. Larger than me. It's sort of like when there is a remake of a classic (like, say, the movie *Dirty Dancing*), and everyone sort of groans because nothing beats the original, you know?

There is always a level of apprehension, like *What if I screw them up? What if I ruin this perfect thing?* Of course, I know they aren't perfect. I do know this. But it's still hard to touch something so well-loved. To try and capture everything they were ten years ago and blend it with the parents and husbands they are now.

I did my best with *#ManLove,* wanting to bring an update to the family we love and celebrate Trent & Drew as they should be celebrated. It was good to be back in that world again, to see them and to watch Trent & Drew be amazing dads.

I wanted to do something special for the cover too. Since writing *#Junkie,* character art has exploded onto the scene, becoming SO popular—for good reason! I have art for all of my *Westbrook* couples and two pieces for Romeo and Rimmel. But up until now, we didn't have any art for Trent and Drew. I think David DaSilva captured them beautifully with his custom art. The coloring, the attention to detail. The way they look at each other. It embodies them. And I mean, the Fastback!

I think turning it into a whole scene from their newest *GearShark* photoshoot was so fun, and I snickered the whole time thinking about Trent with his shirt open and Drew having a fit about it. Marisa at Cover Me Darling, of course, brought it all together with the magazine-style design and text!

Special thanks to everyone who has opened their hearts to Trent & Drew and supported me when I said I was writing their book and still supports me today. *#ManLove* is just as much for you as it is for them. After all, we wouldn't still be obsessing over and loving them a *decade* later if you didn't keep them in your hearts.

Who knows what the next ten years have in store for this family? But I do know one thing for absolute certain: They will all be together. #trewlove forever.

If you enjoyed *#ManLove,* please leave a review online. Reviews help!

Thank you for reading. I appreciate you.

See you next book!

~XO~
Cambria

ABOUT CAMBRIA HEBERT

Cambria Hebert is a bestselling novelist of more than seventy titles. She went to college for a bachelor's degree, couldn't pick a major, and ended up with a degree in cosmetology. So rest assured her characters will always have good hair.

Besides writing, Cambria loves a pumpkin spice latte, staying up late, sleeping in, and watching K drama until her eyes won't stay open. She considers math human torture and has an irrational fear of chickens (yes, chickens). You can often find her running on the treadmill (she'd rather be eating a donut), painting her toenails (because she bites her fingernails), or walking her chihuahuas (the real bosses of the house).

Cambria has written in many genres, including new adult, sports romance, male/male romance, sci-fi, thriller, suspense, contemporary romance, and young adult. Many of her titles have been translated into foreign languages and have been the recipient of multiple awards.

Awards Cambria has received include:

Author of the Year 2016 (UtopiaCon2016)
The Hashtag Series: Best Contemporary Series of 2015 (UtopiaCon 2015)
#Nerd: Best Contemporary Book Cover of 2015 (UtopiaCon 2015)
Romeo from the Hashtag Series: Best Contemporary Lead (UtopiaCon 2015)
#Nerd: Top 50 Summer Reads (Buzzfeed.com 2015)
The Hashtag Series: Best Contemporary Series of 2016 (UtopiaCon 2016)
#NERD Book Trailer: Best Book Trailer of 2016 (UtopiaCon 2016)
#Nerd Book Trailer: Top 50 Most Cinematic Book Trailers of All Time (film-14.com)
#Nerd: Book Most Wanted to be Adapted to Screen (2018)
Amnesia: Mystery Book of the Year (2018)
Red: Best LGBTQIA+ Book of the Year (2022)

Cambria Hebert owns and operates Cambria Hebert Books, LLC.

You can find out more about Cambria and her titles by visiting her website:
http://www.cambriahebert.com

Stay up to date on all of Cambria's new releases and more by signing up for her newsletter: https://view.flodesk.com/pages/62bf54af9b2a0dd45de3fa82

www.ingramcontent.com/pod-product-compliance
Lightning Source LLC
Chambersburg PA
CBHW030334310726
48979CB00001B/22

* 9 7 8 1 9 4 6 8 3 6 8 4 7 *